The Wagon

Stu Campbell

ISBN: 978-0-9988499-4-2

6   5   4   3   2   1

Edited by Mira Perrizo
Cover and text design by D.K. Luraas
Cover painting by R. Loren Schmidt

Printed in the United States of America

ONE

The bulls weren't moving well. There was a lot of fighting among them. Warnings came from all the hands, "Watch out!" or "Give 'em plenty of room!" The warnings were well heeded. When a bull gets beaten in a fight with another bull, he'll be mad and take it out on anything that's close, be it a man on horseback or a sagebrush.

"Them bulls all seem to be on the fight," said Jim.

"They know where they're goin' an' I suppose they're tryin' to establish dominance early," said Chet.

"But it's spring. I'd think they'd be in a better mood knowin' where they're goin' an' what their job is," replied Jim.

"I don't suppose they're thinkin' ahead," said Chet. "We all need to be careful or somebody will get up-ended by one of 'em."

Chet was the cow boss on a fairly large cow

outfit. He'd decided to take the bulls to the cows on this day. The bulls had wintered on the hay fields close to the home ranch. It was the middle of June and he was figuring on starting the calving around the middle of March next year. There were about fifty bulls in the herd.

I figured the outfit had around a thousand head of cows, one bull to every twenty or twenty-five cows. The cows were already on the summer range and they were well scattered. We'd been out on the wagon, branding calves since the first of April.

The wagon wasn't really a horse-drawn wagon. Our bedrolls and groceries and supplies were hauled to our camp in a pickup. It was a term that had been handed down over the years from the late eighteen-hundreds. We were doing things just as they had back then. If a feller said we were going out on the pickup, nobody would know what he was talking about and would probably figure we were going for a Sunday afternoon joy ride. Some things don't change over the years, but in some ways, they do.

Counting the cow boss, there were eight of us buckaroos on the wagon and one rep from a neighboring outfit. The rep was there to look out for his outfit's interest, and make sure we didn't brand any of their calves.

There was a cook back at camp and a horse wrangler out watching the cavy. The horse wrangler was a youngster, just out of high school and learning how to buckaroo. Each one of the buckaroos had a string of five or six horses, and the horses that weren't being used needed to be watched or they'd go back to the home ranch— life was a little easier there and a horse didn't have to look far for his feed.

Moving the bulls was slow. They didn't move as fast as the cows and with all the fighting, it didn't speed things up. When we finally reached the gate to the summer range, I thought we'd be done, but the cow boss wanted to take them farther onto the range. So we kept pushing the herd west.

The summer range was large. It was mostly sagebrush with a sprinkling of cedar and piñon trees. There were a few creeks where the cattle could water. Grass was scarce, scattered among the sagebrush. There weren't really any mountains close, but the sagebrush-covered hills were fairly steep in some areas. Snow-covered mountains could be seen in the distance. There were no pine trees in the area. I don't know the elevation, but the nights were cool and the days were becoming hot. There were no roads past the camp. This was as close to wilderness as there could be. Deer were scarce, although they generally moved out when the cows came. We'd see one occasionally, but not for long.

Moving the herd of bulls became slower as the day heated up. They were all in good shape and too fat to move fast. As the day heated up, the bull fights became more frequent.

Soon we started seeing cows with branded calves. We'd already branded these calves, but there were a lot more to brand farther out on the range.

At one point, Rod got too close to a couple of bulls fighting and the loser of the fight started after Rod and his horse. We all paused to see who would win the race, the bull or the horse. If the bull won and upended Rod's horse, it could leave Rod in a very dangerous position—on the ground, afoot, with a mad bull wanting to take out his frustration on anything handy.

Chet started toward where Rod was having his problem as fast as he could, but Rod's horse quickly out-distanced the bull.

Chet and Rod rode back to the herd. "That was a fool stunt you pulled," said Chet.

"Well, I was just tryin' to move them bulls back to the herd," replied Rod.

"You need to be more careful," said Chet. "We can't afford to get anybody hurt out here. There ain't no roads or ambulance service out here in case somebody gets seriously hurt."

Rod didn't have a reply.

"We've only got a mile or so till we can leave the bulls on water an' head back to camp."

As cow boss, Chet was not only responsible for the cattle, but also the horses and the welfare of the hands. If someone got seriously hurt, he'd have to get them back to camp, if he could, then take them to the home ranch in the pickup. If they were hurt to the point where they couldn't be moved, he'd have to go to camp then to the home ranch and call for a helicopter to take the injured buckaroo to town. Town was about a hundred miles away.

It took an hour to get the bulls to the water. There were some cows on the water.

"We can leave 'em here, boys. They can scatter themselves an' we'll help 'em a little tomorrow. I think it's time we got back to camp an' had some supper."

We rode back to camp at a good, fast trot. Other than when we were moving cattle, all our riding was done at a trot. We'd start out in the morning at a trot and keep it up until the cow boss started sending each one of us out to gather cattle in different directions. He'd send us out with instructions as to where we'd meet with the cattle we'd gathered to hold our branding. We'd brand, earmark, castrate, and vaccinate all the calves. There would be two men on the ground working the calves, two men in the herd roping, and the rest would be outside the herd, keeping it in check. Everyone would have a chance to rope on different days. The cow boss was good at giving everyone an opportunity to rope.

Of course, roping was the most fun. Occasionally, the cow boss would take a turn at roping, but not too often. He knew how to keep his crew happy.

Some of the hands would fall asleep while day-herding the herd. A loud holler would generally wake them up when a cow or two was trying to escape. When the yelling didn't wake up the hand, whoever was closest would turn the cattle back to the herd. I never could figure how they could sleep horseback and not fall off. I've tried it, but could never fall asleep.

Our camp was located alongside a river. The water ran cold under the surface. There were no trees close to camp. Camp consisted of a large tent for sleeping and a smaller tent where the cook worked and slept. Actually, it was very comfortable. The cook did a good job and even made sweet rolls on occasion.

The day would start early. The cow boss would generally be the first one up. He'd wake up the horse wrangler and the horse wrangler would gather the cavy from a fenced night pasture. While the wrangler was gathering the cavy, the rest of the hands would eat breakfast.

The horse wrangler would bring the cavy to a rope corral and the cow boss would rope everyone's horse out. Only the cow boss would be in the rope corral, too many people could cause the horses to break out.

When a buckaroo was given his horse for the day by the cow boss, he'd take him away from the rope corral, hobble him and saddle him. Some of the horses didn't like being saddled and they'd buck a little.

The cow boss would be the last one to saddle up and when he was mounted, we'd head out at a fast trot. The horse wrangler would let the cavy out and day herd them until supper time.

It was a pretty good life. There wasn't any radio or television, we were free from the distractions of everyday life that city people had to deal with. It was a simple life.

One day, the cow boss sent me off first to gather cows. "Push those cows up the draw," he said. "Stan will meet you part way up the draw an' help you bring 'em to the brandin' grounds." He gave me directions on where to drive the cows I found. I started out and the first cattle I came to included a spotted-face cow.

I had a hard time pushing the cattle up the draw and was wishing Stan would show up quickly. But he didn't show. I finally managed to get to the branding grounds only to find all the hands there, already started with the branding.

I took a position outside the herd that I'd added the cattle I found and the cow boss came up to me and said, "I thought you'd got lost an' was thinkin' we'd have to hunt for you."

"I did have some trouble comin' up the draw," I said. "Never did see Stan."

"When Stan came in without you, I thought you'd bucked off your horse or somethin'," replied the cow boss. "But I recognized the spotted-face cow an' knew you were comin'. Stan don't have much patience."

"With all the trouble I was havin', I was hopin' he'd show up. I sure could have used some help. It was tough goin'," I said. I was going to add, "Why do you keep him on? He spends a lot of the time herdin' while sleepin'," but decided to keep my mouth shut. Stan knew more about these fellers than I did and he'd worked with some of them before. I certainly didn't want to cause any trouble and be out-numbered on this outfit.

I gave the cow boss the blackleg vaccine. I was the only one that had saddlebags and had been selected to carry the medicine each day. Chet took the vaccine and without saying anything returned to the branding fire. I took a position outside the herd to help contain the cattle. I was kinda upset at Stan for not waiting for me, or even coming to look for me when I was late, but decided not to say anything. That was the cow boss's job. I figured I'd at least shown everyone what a good hand I was. I did take a lot of pride in being a good hand.

Most of the time we were done sometime in the early afternoon. We'd generally have a little time before supper to catch up on some sleep. I never could figure out how those guys that slept in the saddle while on the day herding could sleep during the late afternoon, but they managed to do it.

One day Stan's horse came unglued and fell over backward and kind of to the right side. Stan cleared his stirrups and managed to almost clear himself from the fallen horse, but not completely. He had his right foot caught under the horse. The horse struggled to get up, but Stan kept his head turned toward him and kept him down. He had to make sure he'd cleared his right stirrup.

Al, a close friend of Stan's, was already on his horse, but came over fast, leaped off his horse and got Stan's horse's head and held him down.

"Is my foot clear of the stirrup?" asked Stan. He sounded kinda worried.

"Can't tell," answered Al. "We'll have to let him up, slowly, an' check. I'll keep hold of his head."

Al let the horse get up. Stan's foot was clear of the stirrup, and as soon as he could, Stan rolled out of the way. But not before the horse kicked him in the leg.

The horse got all the way up and tried to get away, but Al kept a good hold on him. He bucked a couple of times then simmered down.

Still holding the horse, Al went over to where Stan was trying to get up. Chet and Jim were already there, helping Stan up.

"You okay?" asked Jim.

"Of course not," answered Stan. "My horse just fell on me! An' he kicked me to boot!"

"Can you walk?" asked Chet.

"I think so," replied Stan, as he gingerly took a step on his right leg. He tried it again, then took a few more steps. "I'm all right. Just kinda tender."

Paul had caught Al's horse. He'd been wandering loose around camp. Al didn't have time to hobble him in his rush to help Stan.

Al gave Stan's horse to him and took his own horse from Paul. "Thanks," he said. He got on his horse then moved closer to Stan's horse where Stan was getting ready to mount.

"You want me to snub him?" he asked Stan.

"No," answered Stan.

But Al kept his horse close to Stan's just in case the horse came unglued again. Stan was older and did have some difficulty getting on, but he got on without incident.

When the hands were mounted, Chet looked everyone over, got on his own horse and we started out.

I'd been some distance away from where the action with Stan was happening. I was on my own horse and trying to get closer to the action to be of whatever help I could, but Stan's struggling horse spooked my horse and I couldn't get him close. When Stan's horse settled down, my horse got over his fear and I rode close to the action. I put my horse on the off side of Stan's just to help Stan's horse stand still while Stan got on.

We rode out at a slow trot, set by the cow boss, probably for Stan's benefit, and started gathering cattle. The day proceeded much like the others and when we were done and back in camp, I noticed that Al put his horse in a position to keep Stan's horse relatively still while Stan got off.

Stan got off and limped over to the cook's tent after he'd unsaddled and turned his horse loose.

As Stan limped past me, I said, "Got a hitch in your get-along, huh." It was more of a statement than a question.

"Just a little stiff," replied Stan. "It'll be okay in a day or so."

At bedtime that night, Stan showed us his leg. It was black and blue with a kind of yellowed impression of a horseshoe in the center. It didn't look good. I thought it must be quite painful, although Stan didn't complain.

The next few days were uneventful. We did

have rain one day and couldn't brand, so we packed salt.

While gathering cattle, we saw wild horses quite often. On the way back to camp, sometimes we'd give them a run, hoping to catch one. We were unsuccessful, but had a lot of fun. Most of the time we only saw their rear ends as they ran over the next ridge after they spotted us.

On one of these chases, Paul followed a couple of two-year-olds that splintered off from the bunch.

We met at a pre-designated location. The mustangs had been run so much before that Chet, Jim, and Al knew which way they were going to run when they were started.

"Where's Paul?" someone asked.

"Don't know. He started out after them two colts that run off," answered Chet. "He'll show up, or his horse will. We'll look for him later."

Paul was late getting back to camp and was missing his rope when he got there.

"What happened?" asked Chet.

"I caught one of those rangs," replied Paul, "but couldn't get my dallies an' lost my rope. You got an extra one?"

"Nope," answered Chet.

I overheard the conversation and thought, *Well, that'll give everyone an extra chance to rope.*

"That means there's a broomtail out there draggin' a rope around," said Jim. "He'll be easy to follow, but he'll probably get the rope caught on somethin' an' choke himself to death. Someday, probably, some ol' waddy will come across a skeleton with a rope on him. Then, your rope will be found. No tellin' where you'll be." Jim smiled as he said that.

"That ain't funny!" said Paul. "I don't like the idea of a wild horse out there chokin' hisself to death."

"Then you shouldn't have roped him," countered Jim, his smile gone. Jim was bracing himself for a confrontation.

"What's goin' on here?" asked Chet.

"Jim's makin a joke of that wild horse out there probably chokin' hisself to death," said Paul.

"You probably shouldn't have roped him," replied Chet.

"That's what Jim said!" replied Paul.

"Well, it's true," said Chet. "You'd have been better off if you'd have had someone else out there to help you."

"When are we goin' to look for him an' get my rope back?" asked Paul.

"We ain't," replied Chet.

"We ain't?" questioned Paul, somewhat astonished. "But he'll die out there!"

"That's too bad," answered Chet. "But we got plenty of work with the brandin' yet."

"But he'll die out there!" repeated Paul.

"Listen, son, that rang's only worth twenty maybe twenty-five dollars at the most," said Chet. "It ain't worth the time. If you want to get your rope back, the best thing to do is take a rifle an' shoot him. That'll be the easiest an' best way to get your rope back."

"I can't do that," stated Paul. "I didn't intend to kill the horse!"

"It's as good as done," said Chet. "Might just as well forget it."

Paul went to bed that night bewildered and disappointed.

The next day we came across the same bunch of wild horses we'd run the day before. Chet held a conference and he, Jim, and Al decided which way the horses would run if we chased them. After giving instructions on how to head the horses to everyone and telling us not to start until he, Jim, and Al got into the best position to rope the broomtail that was dragging Paul's rope.

It took them about an hour to get into position.

They took the long way, not wanting to be spotted by the wild horses. When we finally saw them get to where they wanted to be—in a saddle on the ridge—the rest of us started toward the mustang bunch as directed.

TWO

There were only about six mares with three young colts. There were a couple of yearlings, a couple of two-year-olds and, of course, the stud. The stud wasn't a beautiful example of horseflesh like the movies portray. He was a blue roan with a lot of scars from fights with other stallions while trying to keep his harem intact. He was missing part of his left ear and had probably got it bitten off in a fight with another stud. Apparently, he'd won enough fights to keep six mares.

The yearlings were blue roans, as were the two-year-olds. That told me that the blue stud had been in charge of this bunch probably for the last three years. Of the three young colts, one was a blue roan, one was a paint, and one was a bay. I figured the blue roan colt was definitely the stud's and it was hard to tell where the paint and bay colt came from. I pondered the question as we chased the wild horses up to the saddle on the ridge.

The colts could have been the blue stud's or he could have stolen the already pregnant mares from another stud bunch. I smiled as I thought, *I'll never know.*

The wild horses were winded when they reached the saddle on the ridge and, as it was told to me, Jim didn't have a problem getting his rope on the horse that was dragging Paul's rope. Al roped the horse's hind feet and they had the horse stretched out on the ground. Chet was pulling hairs from the horse's tail. They were castrating the colt and Chet would use the tail hairs to tie off the cords. Paul's rope was already off the horse and lying on the ground.

"You got my rope back," said Paul.

"Yep," said Chet as he continued the operation.

"Can I give you a hand there?" questioned Paul as he got off his horse to get his rope.

"Nope," replied Chet.

When Chet finished, he asked Paul, "Do you want this rang?"

"I don't have a horse trailer or any way to take him anywhere. I thought I'd give him to the company," said Paul.

"Well, you caught him on company time so

technically he belongs to the company," said Chet. "We'll cross hobble him an' take him home. Besides, that saves me the trouble of sending you a bill for castrating him." Chet had a smile when he added his last comment.

"What do you mean, cross hobble?" asked Paul. His inexperience was showing.

"We'll tie the left front foot to the right rear foot with just enough slack to allow the horse to move," replied Chet. "Jim, you keep your rope on his neck when we let him up. He'll figure out how to move before too long so you'll keep him in check."

Jim nodded knowingly. I got the idea they'd done this before.

"Seein' as we got your rope back, we'll use it to hobble this broomtail," said Chet.

"Sure," said, Paul as he handed the rope to Chet.

I smiled at Paul's willingness to let Chet use his rope. Again, his inexperience was showing. The knots Chet had to tie in the rope to make hobbles would put kinks in the hard twist rope and it would be pretty much worthless. But Paul was willing.

"Al, give him some slack an' let him up. We better get goin' or we'll be late for supper."

Al unwrapped his rope from the saddle horn and moved his horse forward. The blue got to his feet and tried to get away, but after his operation, he didn't have much fight. Jim kept him under control.

Chet got on his horse, took down his rope, and said, "Jim, you lead. Maybe he'll follow. You boys ride along each side. I'll follow an' keep him movin'."

It was slow going back to camp with the mustang hobbled as he was. Chet used his rope when the wild horse balked and the colt threw himself a number of times. Even though he'd been castrated, he still put up a pretty fair fight.

After a mile or so, Jim stopped. "If I make a halter out of this rope, we'll have him broke to lead by the time we get to camp." Jim fashioned a halter out of his lariat and with some convincing, the blue colt was persuaded to follow Jim's horse.

We made better time when the blue colt started to lead, but were still late getting into camp. I really appreciated the fact that we generally trotted at a pretty good pace back to camp when we were done with the day's work. Going at a walk just made the day longer.

When we reached camp, John, the cook,

was sitting outside his tent. "You boys are late today. The horse wrangler has already ate and turned the horses out," he said, as we unsaddled our horses and turned them loose in the night pasture.

"We picked up an extra horse," said Chet. "He kinda slowed us down as we taught him some manners. Leave the hobbles on the rang until he learns he's supposed to stay with the cavy. It'll take a few days. Let's eat! I ain't had nothin' since breakfast!"

"Supper's ready," said John. "The taters are overdone, but they're hot. I'll cook your steaks to order, so you guys that want your steaks well done will get them last."

We all filed into the tent, got plates and started eating taters while the steaks were cooking.

John was an exceptional camp cook. He managed to cook everyone's steak to order and cooked eggs to order in the morning. He even made sweet rolls on occasion. He was probably the main reason everyone got along as well as they did in camp.

One day, while all the buckaroos were out, Matt, the ranch foreman, showed up at camp. He brought more groceries for the cook, cigarettes for the hands that needed them, and mail for those that had received mail. He was still in camp when we returned. The cigarettes were brought out by the carton and the price was deducted from the buckaroo's pay. The ranch actually had a small store where all the hands could buy cigarettes, shaving supplies, and miscellaneous items.

Chet and Matt were discussing how the branding was coming along. I overheard them and Chet told Matt that he figured we'd be done by the fourth of July.

"A few days of ridin', gatherin' the yearlin's, an' we'll pretty much be done," said Chet.

"You'll probably have a bunch of hungover buckaroos after the fourth," said Matt.

"It happens every year," replied Chet. "But, we'll manage."

"How many calves you got branded so far?" asked Matt.

Chet took out his tally book and checked his figures. "I ain't got it totaled," he said, "but I figure we're brandin' somewheres between thirty an' fifty calves a day."

Matt looked over the figures in the tally book. "Then you're a little over half done," said Matt.

"Yep. We'll be done by the fourth."

Matt turned to the rest of the buckaroos that

were gathered around getting ready for supper. "Any of you boys need anything? I'll be back in about ten days."

The hands put in their orders and Matt left.

The next few days were uneventful. We did come across another bunch of mustangs and tried to catch them, but without success. Actually, we did have some success. A young colt became separated from his mother and followed Vince's horse back toward camp. The colt was clearly lost.

"Looks like you've got a baby to care for," Chet told Vince.

"Yeah," stated Vince. "But I don't need him."

A few attempts to separate the colt from Vince were unsuccessful.

"Looks like we'll have to use more drastic measures," said Chet. "You head back to the area where the colt got separated an' I'll try an' convince him to stay in that area. We'll run him till he gets tired, then leave him."

"Okay," replied Vince and he started back. The rest of us buckaroos headed toward camp at a slow trot, wanting to give Chet and Vince a chance to catch up.

When they did catch up to us, Paul fell in beside Chet.

"What'll happen to that colt?" Paul asked.

"Nothin'," answered Chet.

"Won't he starve out here without his ma?"

"Nope."

"How come?" asked Paul.

"He'll find his mother."

"How?" asked Paul.

"He'll go back to where he last sucked an' find his ma there," answered Chet. "He'll be all right. You seem to have a lot of concern for these rangs."

"Yep," replied Paul.

It was Chet's turn to ask questions. "How come?"

"They're a big part of our American heritage," replied Paul. "They're a symbol. I think they should be our national animal." Paul made a good argument for the wild horses.

"No," countered Chet. "They're worthless. They eat up a lot of the feed an' they keep the cattle off the water. They're inbred an' most of 'em are crooked legged. The whole country would be better off without 'em."

"I don't think you like 'em very much," stated Paul.

"You're right there!" Chet turned and left.

Jim was listening to this conversation and as

Chet passed him, he said, "Paul seems to think a lot of them ol' broomtails."

"Yeah," said Chet. "He's an individualistic daydreamer! Don't have no sense."

Paul wasn't making any progress with Chet. I overheard the conversation and said to Paul as he left, "I think I'd not say anythin' to Chet in the future 'bout them mustangs. Best to stay on the good side of him."

Paul didn't say anything but he left clearly upset and I heard him muttering something about, "Them uncivilized savages! They ain't got no feelin's for anythin'! This is a blood-thirsty outfit!"

As the days passed, Paul became more sullen and glum. The only one in camp he would talk to at night was the horse wrangler.

The horse wrangler was a teenager, fresh out of high school. I presumed he'd graduated, but he could have quit school early, I never did find out. He seemed to be a pretty good kid. There was always a smile on his face and he seemed to be happy-go-lucky. His name was William and he preferred that to Bill.

I was concerned that Paul was spending a lot of time with William and thought that Paul might be influencing him in a negative manner.

I didn't like that, but there wasn't anything I could do about it.

I mentioned it to Chet one day. "Don't you think William's spendin' a lot of time with Paul?"

"I noticed that," answered Chet. "Jim mentioned the same thing last night."

"It ain't none of my business," I said, "but I don't think he's a good influence on William."

"You're right there, Kenty boy," said Chet. "Seems like there's a bad apple in every bunch an' Paul's the one here. I wouldn't be surprised if he rolled up an' left. His attitude ain't been right since he got here."

Chet had given me a nickname, Kenty. He only used it when he was in a good mood.

"I ain't tryin' to cause trouble," I said. "But I am concerned about William."

"I know," said Chet. "I'll talk to William sometime in the next couple of days. I don't think it would do any good to talk to Paul."

Chet didn't get a chance to talk to William. The next morning, while roping out everyone's horse, Paul told the cow boss, "I think I need to roll up today."

"I can't take you back to the ranch today," said Chet. "There's too much to do. But if you don't want to work today, you stay in camp an' I'll take you to the ranch this afternoon."

"We can't go now?" queried Paul.

"Nope, unless you want to walk," was Chet's curt reply. "I'll take you back when we get done today. I'm runnin' a cow camp here, not a taxi service to the home ranch. You wait in camp. You can keep the cook company."

Before we left camp that morning, Chet told the cook, "Paul's leavin' this afternoon. You kinda keep an eye on him an' make sure he don't borrow anybody's stuff. Somehow, I don't trust him a hundred percent."

John gave Chet a knowing nod and said, "I'll do it."

When we left camp that morning, Paul wasn't with us. There was a relaxed feeling among the hands that morning. For the last few days there seemed to be an uneasy feeling about everyone.

"Funny how one hand's leavin' the outfit has an effect on everyone," said Rod.

"He sure wasn't a positive factor in this camp," stated Jim.

Vince said, "He told me he was thinkin' of leavin' an' tried to get me to go with him."

"Why didn't you?" Jim asked jokingly.

"I ain't no quitter!" replied Vince. "Besides that, I didn't much like him. He was too much of an idealist for me. An' he was always kinda negative. An', to boot, I kinda like it here."

"He'll be gone this afternoon," said Chet. "As far as I'm concerned, he's history."

We finished the branding later that day. On the way back to camp, Chet told everyone, "Soon as you turn your horses loose, check through your belongin's an' make sure you ain't missin' anything. I'll take Paul to the home ranch an' I'll be back."

John went to Chet and said, "He's good to go. I watched him all day and he couldn't have gone to the bathroom without me knowin'. I even accompanied him in the tent, actin' like I was tryin' to make conversation. That was the sour part of today. All he did was complain an' gripe about this outfit. How'd you guys ever get along with him? I'll be glad when he's gone."

"He was a sour apple on this outfit," replied Chet. "Where's he at now?"

"He's loadin' his stuff in the truck," answered John. "All he's got is a saddle an' a bedroll."

"Good! I'll check with the boys an' we'll get rid of him," said Chet. "I'll be late gettin' back, keep some supper hot for me."

"You ain't goin' to eat at the ranch?"

"Nope," answered Chet. "I ain't goin' all the way to the ranch."

Chet checked with all the hands. Nobody was missing anything. He told Paul, "Get in the truck! We're goin'."

Chet got in the truck and started off before Paul even had the door closed. Chet obviously wasn't too happy.

THREE

We ate supper without Chet that night. The conversation centered on Paul and his leaving.

"I'm glad he's gone," said William. "I didn't much like him. He was always tryin' to partner up with me. I don't need a partner like that."

John asked, "Chet said he wasn't goin' to the ranch, so where's he goin?"

Jim and Rod laughed. Finally Rod said, "Chet'll take him as far as the gate to the hay fields an' let him go there. When the ranch foreman sees him walkin' in carryin' his saddle an' bedroll, he'll know he was fired. Nobody will offer to help him get to town."

"They won't even offer him supper," added Jim, laughing.

"It's kinda a signal between the cow boss an' the foreman that the hand has been fired," chimed in Rod.

Jim, Al, Stan, and Rod had worked for Chet

many times out on the wagon before and they knew what was happening.

"Has this happened much before?" I asked. Vince, William, and I were the only hands that hadn't worked on this outfit before.

"It didn't happen at all last year," said Stan. "The year before, Chet run off two hands. That was a tough year bein' shorthanded. I didn't think we were ever goin' to get done."

"Yeah," said Rod. "It was pretty tough until Matt got a couple of drifters to come out an' help. But it was tough goin' until they came. They weren't much as far as buckaroos are concerned, they couldn't ride very good an' they couldn't anticipate a cow's move, but they did pretty good holdin' the cattle. At least they didn't fall asleep like Stan does an' let cattle get behind 'em."

"Go to blazes!" said Stan. Everyone laughed.

"I only let them cattle behind me to keep you guys an' my horse awake," continued Stan.

"But it ain't right that you should get all the sleep durin' the day while the rest of us is awake," said Rod.

Everyone laughed again. At least this was good-natured ribbing and not taken seriously by Stan or anyone else. Every time someone had tried to rib or tease Paul, he would go on the defensive and wanted to argue with the tormentor. A few times, it almost came to punches until everyone learned to leave him alone. Nobody was afraid of him, but it wasn't a good idea to start something while out on the wagon. It was good he was gone, everyone was a little more relaxed in camp.

Chet returned and while he was eating his supper, Vince asked him, "Did you go to the ranch?"

"No," replied Chet.

Everyone knew where he'd let Paul out.

"I saw him luggin' his saddle an' bedroll toward the ranch in the mirrors when I turned around. He'll probably get to the ranch after dark. He's got a long walk back. When Matt sees him come walkin' in, he'll start lookin' for another hand to help us finish up. Until then, we'll just do whatever we can. We've still got about a month before we're finished. "

There wasn't much more talk of Paul on the wagon.

"What you goin' to do with his string of horses?" asked Vince.

"They'll be all right," answered Chet. "Why do you ask?"

"I kinda took a likin' to that horse of his he

called Hondo. I'd like to trade him for the horse in my string we call Jackknife. He's the hardest ridin' horse I ever been on. His trot is so rough, I've 'bout givin' up eatin' breakfast."

"You want Hondo?" asked Chet.

"Yep," replied Vince.

"He's been known to buck some an' when he bucks it ain't pretty."

"I never saw him buck with Paul," stated Vince.

"The Good Lord looks out for fools an' idiots," said Chet.

"I still think I could get along good with that horse, even without the Good Lord's help," said Vince.

Chet laughed and said, "Okay, I'll trade you if you want, but you need to watch him! You never know when he'll blow up."

Vince asked, "Can I use him tomorrow?"

"I don't see why not," answered Chet. "But don't be afraid to ask for an' accept the Good Lord's help if He offers it." Chet was still grinning as he made his last statement.

The next day, after everyone had saddled their horses, we were watching as Vince saddled Hondo. Rod and Jim were already mounted and had their horses topped off.

Hondo was a little hard to get on. He'd move away from a feller as the feller tried to put his foot in the stirrup. Rod knew this about the horse and moved his horse to the off side of Hondo so he couldn't move away from Vince.

"Just thought I'd like the view over here better," said Rod as Vince gave him a questioning look.

"I never figured you to be the Good Lord," said Vince as he put his foot in the stirrup and swung on. "But I'll accept your help!"

The horse jumped forward as Vince got in the saddle. He couldn't move sideways because Rod and his horse were in the way. Hondo took another jump forward but Rod and his horse were crowding him and he couldn't do much.

Vince pulled the horse's head up and he stopped trying to buck. Jim had moved in close to the near side of Hondo and Jim and Rod almost had him boxed in.

"Well," said Vince, "we'll make a better horse out of you sooner or later!"

We started out that morning at a leisurely trot, as we did every morning. Starting out this way gave the horses a chance to warm up. The day proceeded much like every other day. Chet sent the riders off in different directions with instructions as to where we'd meet with the cattle we'd gathered.

When we'd all gathered at the branding grounds, Chet selected Vince and Rod to rope. Rod was a good roper and didn't miss many loops. Vince wasn't as good as Rod, but he caught a sizeable number of calves.

All went well until Vince had a calf slip behind him and get the rope under Hondo's tail. Vince was just getting his dallies as the calf went down, tightening the rope. Hondo reacted.

Hondo, like most horses, clamped his tail down tight when he felt the rope under his tail. At the same time, he jumped straight up in the air. I was watching and if I was telling the story, I'd say Hondo's feet were ten feet up in the air. But it was actually more like six feet. Regardless, it was a mighty big jump.

Vince was loosened on that first jump and when Hondo reached the peak and started down, Vince kept going. Vince's feet were about ten feet off the ground when he started down.

The calf was dragged a few feet until the rope came out from under Hondo's tail. With the rope free from Hondo, the calf kicked free from the rope and ran back to the herd. I don't know if the calf wanted to get back to the safety of the herd, or was just trying to get away from Hondo and possible injury from Hondo's actions.

Hondo was bucking hard and apparently not watching where he was going. His second jump was just about as high as his first and as he reached the top of it, he turned his belly to the sun, almost turning upside down.

I remember thinking, *A sun fisher,* and thought of the old song, "The Strawberry Roan." In that song, the roan is "a sun-fishing son-of-a-gun."

Hondo took another jump almost as high as the first two and when he came down, he landed on top of a cow. That tipped him over and he fell on his side. He scrambled up and was still bucking when he got to his feet.

Cows were scattering everywhere. Rod had his rope down, made a loop and made a good throw toward Hondo. His loop was true and he had the horse. He took his dallies and when Hondo hit the end of the rope, he was in the middle of another jump. The rope tightened and Hondo almost pulled Rod's horse over. But Rod's horse maintained his balance.

When the rope tightened, Hondo was pulled over and landed on the ground on his back. Hondo scrambled to his feet and Rod took advantage of the slack in the rope, shortened the lead and dallied again. He had Hondo on a pretty short lead and Hondo couldn't make his big jumps. But he continued to try and buck.

Cattle were still scattering and I didn't see how Rod got the rope from under Hondo's tail. I found out later that it had come free of its own accord. I had to stop some escaping cattle. They were leaving at a fast trot. If they'd have been running, we'd have had a stampede, but they were just trotting.

I got around the leaders and turned them back toward the herd. I met Jim, coming around the other side.

Jim said, "I'll have to ask Stan if he saw what happened or if he was sleepin'."

"You won't have to wait till we get back to the gather," I said. "He's comin' up behind you pushin' some cows."

"You been sleepin?" asked Stan. "These cows were tryin' to get away."

"No, I ain't been sleepin'," answered Jim. "That's your job!"

"That ain't my job!" exclaimed Stan. "I saw everything. I even saw that you let these cows behind you!"

Stan was always taking some harassment about falling asleep while on day herd. However, the exchange between the two men was cordial.

We pushed the cattle back to the herd. I saw that the rope had come out from under Hondo's tail and the horse had calmed down some. I couldn't see Vince, he was still lying on the ground, apparently in quite a bit of pain.

Al had been helping Chet on the ground and they were both over by Vince.

Chet had already asked Vince if he was all right.

Vince's answer was an adamant, "No!"

"Can you walk?" asked Chet.

"I don't know," replied Vince. "I can't even get up."

"You'll have to try," said Chet. "We can't leave you out here for coyote bait."

With some help from Chet and Al, Vince got to his feet, slowly.

"Where's it hurt?" asked Al.

"My hip's mighty sore," replied Vince. "Where's my horse?"

"Rod's got the horse," said Chet. "Can you walk?"

"Of course," answered Vince. "I been walkin' since I was a little kid!"

Chet smiled. "Give it a try now," he said.

Vince took a very slow step and faltered. Chet and Al helped him maintain his balance. Another step, although unsteady, produced better results.

Watching the situation, I thought Vince might have broken his hip and thought Chet would have to go to the ranch, call into town for an emergency helicopter evacuation to take Vince to the hospital.

But another step and Vince appeared to loosen up a little. Another step was better, although Vince had a noticeable limp. A few more steps and Vince was walking without help from Chet or Al.

"Keep walkin' an' it'll loosen up," said Al.

Vince hobbled around and seemed to be improving. It was his right hip that was giving him problems.

After about twenty minutes, Vince appeared to be better.

"Where's my horse?" he asked.

"Rod's got him over there," answered Chet.

"I think I can get on an' ride," said Vince.

"That's good," said Chet. "It's a long walk back to camp."

Vince struggled over to where Rod had Hondo.

"I'll keep him snubbed up for you," said Rod. "It'll be easier to get on."

"Sure," said Vince.

Slowly and painfully, Vince got on the horse. It sure wasn't graceful.

Chet walked over to Vince, where Rod still had Hondo snubbed and said, "You just watch the herd. I'll have Raymond rope in your place. It'll be easier on you."

Acknowledging that Chet was doing him a favor, Vince simply said, "Thanks."

Raymond was the representative for the neighboring outfit, but Chet gave him an equal chance to rope along with his own buckaroos. Our outfit had sent a rep to the neighbors so it was an equal exchange of help. The job of the rep was to look out for his outfit's interests and make sure his outfit's calves weren't branded with the wrong brand.

We finished branding that day and took a more leisurely ride home. I'm sure that was for Vince's benefit. He was still experiencing a great deal of pain.

We were a little late getting back to camp and after we'd unsaddled our horses and turned them loose, Chet said to Vince, "You go sit in the creek for an hour or so an' soak your hip. The cook will call you when your supper's ready."

Vince did as he was told and we all saw the big black and blue bruise that covered Vince's hip and had started down his leg when he came out of the tent naked.

Chet was looking at Vince's hip and asked him as he entered the water, "Do you want me to take you to the ranch an' have someone run you into the doc? That bruise looks pretty serious. There's kinda a yellow spot in the middle an' I don't think that's good."

"I think it'll be okay," replied Vince. "Let's wait an' see what it's like in the mornin'. That water is cold!"

"Whatever you say," said Chet, laughing. "But don't you keep everyone awake tonight cussin' an' moanin' on account of the pain."

"I'll try not to," laughed Vince.

After a while the cook called Vince to his supper. Vince went to the tent, got dried off, dressed and went to eat. The rest of the hands had already finished supper.

"Where is everybody?" asked Vince as he entered the cook tent.

"They've already et," said the cook. "Chet

wanted me to keep you out in the creek for at least an hour. How's the hip?"

"I think the water helped," replied Vince. "It don't feel too bad now."

"If you want, I'll wake you up when I get up an' you can soak in the creek in the mornin'," volunteered the cook.

"Nope," replied Vince. "It'll be colder in the mornin'. I'll be lucky if I don't catch my death from the cold water tonight."

Vince finished his supper and went straight to bed. The rest of us hands had turned in earlier that night.

During the night, I heard Vince moan a few times as he turned over and that was unusual. I sleep pretty sound and generally don't hear anything during the night. Vince spent a fairly restless night.

The next morning, Chet told Vince, "I need to look at that hip this mornin'."

Vince dropped his drawers to expose his hip. It didn't look any better.

"I'm goin' to take you to the ranch," said Chet. "You need to have a doctor look at that. It don't look any better. I'll bet you can't walk very far on it. You other boys can take a day off in camp. If you want to do laundry, hang it out on the brush to dry. William, you still need to take the horses out to graze. Go get in the truck, Vince. Any of you boys need anything from the ranch? I'll bring it back. If you got any mail to go out, get it ready."

Vince was hobbling toward the truck when Chet got in. Unlike he did when he took Paul in, he waited until Vince got in the truck and closed the door before he started off.

I went back to my bedroll and laid down to relax. The others gathered around and made idle conversation.

Raymond asked, "Will Chet bring Vince back?"

"Nope," answered Jim. "Chet'll be back this afternoon, but someone from the ranch will take Vince to the doc."

FOUR

Chet returned later that day. He had two more hands with him. He introduced them to everyone. One was Roger and the other one was Clark. Both had done some cowboying in the past.

I'd met Clark in the past on another outfit I'd worked for. I didn't know him that well, I only recognized him. At that outfit he was farm help. I didn't figure him to be a cowboy, much less a buckaroo.

Clark showed some sign of recognition as we shook hands. "Didn't you used to work over on the Circle Dot?" he asked.

"Yep," I replied, "but that was a couple of years ago."

"How come you left there?"

"The ridin' job was over an' I wasn't much interested in helpin' out with the hay," I replied. "It was time to move on."

"That was a pretty rough outfit," stated Clark. "A lot of rough characters there."

"Another good reason to move on," I said.

"What's this outfit like?"

"This is a pretty square outfit. Some of the horses are kinda rough, but the cow boss is straight. He's tough, but fair. He don't put up with a lot of foolishness. You an' that other guy, what's his name, Roger? Are you travelin' together?"

"Nope. I never met him till I got to the ranch. Don't know anything about him."

"How'd you get hired on here?" I asked.

"The employment agency sent me to talk to Matt. Matt said one of your hands had got run off an' the cow boss came in with an injured hand. I was there, they asked me if I could ride, I said "some," so Matt had me talk to Chet. I got hired."

"What about Roger?" I asked.

"He'd been there a day or two. Matt hired him to replace the hand that got run off. He was goin' to bring him out in a day or two, then Chet showed up an' brought us both out. I don't know much about him, he didn't talk much comin' out here."

Chet came over while Clark and I were visiting and said, "Get your bedroll an' find a place to bunk in the tent. The saddle I'm lendin' you, it's a company saddle, and you can put it with the others. We'll be startin' early in the mornin' so be ready to go. I think I'll take a little rest before supper."

Roger had already put his bedroll in the tent and was stretched out on it, taking a nap. He'd put his saddle with the others.

The next morning, Chet roped out Jackknife for Clark. I heard Al say to Stan, "I hope that kid can ride. If he can't that horse will jar his innards loose. He's a mighty hard ridin' horse."

"We'll find out," said Stan. "I imagine Chet gave him that horse because he's gentle. A lot of the horses left in the cavy are broncs or colts. I'm thinkin' Chet ain't sure about that feller's abilities. He's usin' a company saddle an' he ain't got no chaps or other equipment. Chet even had to lend him a bit an' hobbles."

"Yeah," said Al.

Chet roped out a horse called Sunset for Roger. Everyone else had their horses saddled and they stopped untracking their horses to watch Roger saddle and mount Sunset. Jim, Rod, and I were already mounted, having already untracked our horses.

Sunset had somewhat of a reputation for

bucking. Rod told me "Sunset had earned his name because he'd put a hand in the hospital and the hand almost died. Sunset, the end of the day. Almost the end of the trail for that feller. Get it?"

I just nodded. I got the correlation.

Roger put his foot in the stirrup. I could see Sunset tense up and knew there was going to be some action.

Roger swung into the saddle and Sunset was already bucking, even though Roger had cheeked the horse. Sunset couldn't get his head down until Roger let the headstall loose and Roger didn't turn the headstall loose until he was in the saddle.

With his head loose, Sunset really turned it on. He drove his head down to the ground and went straight up in the air. His feet were about four feet off the ground. He came down hard, stiff legged. That landing would have jarred any rider loose, but Roger maintained his seat.

Sunset took another high jump and midway, turned to the right. Roger stayed with him. Sunset hit the ground stiff legged again, but failed to jar Roger loose. He took another jump and this time he turned to the left, trying to unseat Roger. It didn't work. Roger was glued to the saddle.

Rod and I were sitting on our horses watching the action. Our horses shied a little when Sunset started bucking, but we both managed to keep them under control.

"That Roger's sure enough a hand," said Rod after he'd calmed his horse down. "Most fellers would have lost the horse after the first jump."

"Yep," I said. "Those first jumps only lasted about three seconds. That Sunset horse is fast."

Jim's horse hadn't reacted to Sunset's bucking and he rode him over to crowd Sunset. When he got close, we all heard Roger yell, "I got him! I got him!"

Jim backed off and gave Sunset room. A few more jumps and some ground shattering landings and Sunset quit bucking and started running.

"He's got a runaway now," said Rod. "You watch, he'll try bucking while he's runnin'."

I watched and that's exactly what Sunset did. But Roger stayed with him all the way.

Roger got the horse running in a circle and gradually he slowed down. When he got back to camp, Sunset was trotting.

"This horse is feelin' a little frisky this mornin'," said Roger. "An' he needs some work on his brakes!"

The horse didn't stop. He was trotting around the rest of the riders.

"While you've got that horse in gear, we better start movin'," said Chet.

We started out at a good-paced trot. Sunset, although he was blowing hard, didn't have any trouble keeping up. He was trotting right alongside Chet's horse.

I heard Roger tell Chet, "This horse has plenty of energy. I might have to make a circle or two around you before he wants to behave."

"You do what you have to do," said Chet.

Roger said, "You ought to give me the big circle today. This horse can take it."

"Sure," said Chet.

We got to where Chet needed to scatter the riders and Roger got the big circle, even though Sunset had already worked up a sweat.

I got the next big circle and Chet sent Clark with me. Occasionally during the morning's gather, I could see Roger. He had Sunset at a trot all morning near as I could tell.

As we approached where we were going to hold our branding, I had a chance to visit with Clark.

I asked him, "How you gettin' along with that horse?"

"He's a good horse," said Clark. "I like him. I'm sure glad he didn't act like Roger's horse this morning!"

"Yep. Roger had a pretty rough horse this morning. You like Jackknife, huh?"

Clark's reply was a simple, "Yep!"

Within a mile of the branding grounds, Roger put his cows with ours and joined us. Roger's cows were tired. They were breathing hard and a lot of them had their tongues hanging out, drooling. Sunset was covered with sweat and the dust had started to cake on his neck, shoulders and flanks. I could see that the horse had been used very hard that morning. I wondered if he would make it through the day.

As we approached the branding grounds, Chet cast a disapproving eye at the cattle that were tired and an even more disapproving eye at Sunset. But he didn't say anything to Roger.

Chet said, "We've got a pretty big gather today. Stan, you an' Al rope first, then we'll switch off. Jim, you give me a hand on the ground."

Clark asked, "What do you want me to do?" Clark's question indicated how green he was.

"You just stay outside the herd an' keep all the cows gathered. We ain't got a corral, so you an' everyone else has to act like a fence. Roger, you need to give your horse a good rest."

"Good," said Clark. "That'll be fun!"

Clark had no idea how boring day herding can be, again indicating how green he was.

Those of us that weren't roping or helping out on the ground took our positions around the herd. I'd never given it any thought before, but I wasn't much more that a fence post while day herding. Neither was everyone else! Clark seemed to be the only one that was enthusiastic about day herding.

After the fire had been built and the irons got hot, the ropers started catching calves.

Clark did a good job day herding. In fact, he did too good a job. If a cow even looked like she wanted to take a step past the imaginary circle Clark had built around the herd, he was turning her back.

I rode over to him and said, "You don't have to keep the cattle so close. Let 'em spread out a little, just don't let any get behind you. You're kinda pushin' the whole herd over on top of them other guys. Give 'em some room."

Clark eased up on his day herding. Soon he would find out how boring it actually was. But he was a new hand, new at buckarooing, and I figured he wanted to impress the cow boss.

When Chet figured about half the calves had been branded, he called Stan and Al in and gave me and Clark a chance to rope. I think he wanted to see how good a roper Clark was. He already knew about me. I sure wasn't as good as some of the other boys, but I could pretty well hold my own.

"Clark," said Chet, "I'll lend you a rope an' you can take a turn at ropin' a few."

After the third calf that I roped had been branded, Chet told me as he returned the iron to the fire, "You better do a good job an' hurry a little. Clark ain't caught a calf yet. We don't want to be here all night."

"I'm doin' the best I can," I said.

"You're doin' okay. You ain't missed one yet."

I was not aware that the ground crew was keeping score. I knew they were watching, but finding out they were keeping score surprised me. I resolved to do better each time I had a turn to rope.

After a time, Chet called Clark in. While Jim branded the calf I'd roped and dragged to the fire, I heard Chet tell Clark, "I haven't roped for a good many days, I think I'll take a turn.

You go back to day herdin'. I'll have Rod come in an' work the ground with Jim. Give me my rope back. It used to be a catch rope, I hope you haven't changed its habits." Chet was smiling as he said that.

Clark said, "Sure."

I'm not sure Clark knew he was being replaced. He should have, he only caught one calf and I'd caught twelve or fifteen.

Clark thanked Chet for letting him try to catch a few and took up a position day herding. Chet was a little surprised that Clark had thanked him!

Chet caught his horse, took the hobbles off him, took down his rope and started to catch calves. Chet was a pretty good roper, but he didn't rope much. He knew that roping was the fun part of being on the wagon and branding and had his buckaroos do most of the roping. He knew how to keep his crew happy and satisfied.

Roger took up a position for day herding. While I was roping, I couldn't see how well he was doing, but no cattle were escaping. I did notice that his horse was getting a well-deserved rest and seemed to be content to stand still.

At one point, I saw that Stan had fallen asleep and Clark did a good job of returning the escaping cattle to the herd. He didn't wake up Stan as he pushed the cattle back.

I mentioned this to Jim when I dragged a calf to the fire.

"It appears he's very considerate of others," said Jim.

I just nodded in agreement.

When we were done, Chet got off his horse, hobbled him and counted the ears. Jim put the fire out and rubbed the irons in the dirt to cool them off. We had to wait after every branding for the irons to cool, we didn't want to burn a horse with hot irons while riding home.

While waiting for the irons to cool, we generally gathered around what was left of the fire and talked about the day's work.

Chet said, "Them calves were pretty wild today. Clark missed so many they got kinda wild after bein' hit alongside the flanks with the rope so much."

Clark got a little red-faced.

"Clark," said Jim, apparently trying to ease Clark's feelings, "you did a pretty good job today. I noticed that you didn't even wake up Stan when you turned those cows back. The rest of us always wake him up when he falls asleep."

"Go to blazes!" exclaimed Stan.

Jim ignored Stan and continued, "While it's nice to be considerate of him when he does that, you really ought to wake him. If he gets too much sleep during the day, he won't be able to sleep at night."

We all laughed and I'm not sure that Clark knew Jim was poking fun at Stan.

Clark said, "Yes sir!"

Stan made the comment, "Don't you pay any attention to him. I appreciate the consideration an' you keep it up. It's about time I got the respect I truly deserve!"

We all laughed at Stan's comment but it left Clark wondering what he should do in the future.

When the irons were cool enough, Chet tied them on his saddle, unhobbled his horse and got on.

Obviously referring to Roger's horse, he said, "We'll take it easy goin' back to camp. It's been a pretty rough day on the horses."

The dust had caked on Sunset and it was pretty thick.

We got back to camp, turned our horses loose and waited for supper. When John was ready, he called us to eat. He asked Roger and Clark how they wanted their steaks, a question that was largely ignored by other camp cooks.

After supper, most of us went to our tent to relax a little before we turned in for the night. Roger didn't. He was missing until it got dark.

When he finally came into the tent, Chet asked him, "Where you been?"

"I took a little walk down along the creek," replied Roger. "I like to take a stroll each evening before turnin' in. Helps me to relax."

Chet didn't say anything, but I noticed him giving Roger a funny look. Whatever Chet was thinking, he seemed to reconsider and went to bed.

The next day, Chet roped out a horse called Zipper for Roger. Zipper was a good-looking horse, but he only stood about thirteen and a half hands tall. He was fast and known to buck. His bucking wasn't as spectacular as Sunset's, but he put everything he had into it. He was so fast, he could slip out from under a rider before the rider knew it and leave him in midair.

Everyone stopped what they were doing to watch Roger get on Zipper. Some of us were already mounted.

Zipper let Roger get on without any trouble, but when Roger cued him to move, he came uncorked. He moved so fast in his bucking I couldn't really keep track of what was happening. Zipper changed directions in midair so fast it seemed like he was going two different directions at the same time. But Roger stayed right with him.

Roger let the horse buck and finally Zipper stopped.

"This horse likes to warm up pretty fast in the mornin'," said Roger.

"He's pretty fast," said Chet.

"Looks like you've sure enough got yourself a bronc stomper," said Rod.

"I think he could ride anythin' on this outfit," volunteered Jim.

"It appears that way," said Chet. He was eyeing Roger carefully as he said that.

Chet caught his horse, saddled him, got on and said, "Let's go!"

The ride was pretty quiet until we got to where Chet needed to scatter riders. He sent Rod and me on the big circle so I don't know where the other riders went.

Rod and I split up and before long, I met Rod pushing cattle toward where we were supposed to meet. We used a different area each day for branding.

Soon we met other riders pushing the cattle they had gathered toward our meeting place. Roger was one of the last riders we met up with.

Again, his horse was covered with sweat and dust.

Vince and Raymond were chosen to rope first. Chet and Jim did the ground work and the rest of us did the day herding. The branding went well that day and before long, we were headed back to camp.

On the way, I heard Chet tell Jim and Rod, "We'll have to move camp, probably day after tomorrow. Our gathers are gettin' farther away from camp each day."

Rod asked, "We goin' up on Indian Creek?"

"Yep," answered Chet.

FIVE

After supper that night Roger went for his little stroll. When he returned to camp, Chet was waiting for him.

"Been out for a little walk?" Chet asked. Chet was pretty close to Roger, almost in his face. Roger was backing up, not wanting to be that close to Chet. But Chet kept pressing him.

"Yep," Roger answered to Chet's question.

"You been drinkin'!" said Chet. It was more of a statement than a question. Chet didn't give Roger a chance to reply, he followed his statement with the question, "Where'd you get it?"

"I ain't been drinkin'," answered Roger.

"You sure have! I can smell it on you!" Chet was getting a little irritated. "Where'd you get it?"

Roger sensed that he'd been found out and decided to come clean. "I had a little nip earlier," he said.

"Where is it?" asked Chet angrily.

"In my saddlebags," answered Roger.

"Get it!" ordered Chet.

By this time, all the other buckaroos had gathered around after hearing the loud voices.

Meekly, Roger went to his saddle and brought out a pocket flask and handed it to Chet.

"Is this all?" asked Chet.

"Well, no," replied Roger.

"Bring the rest!" ordered Chet.

Again Roger went to his saddle and this time he brought out a fifth of Old Crow whiskey. It was wrapped in a towel to keep it from breaking. He handed it to Chet.

"I'm goin' to give you a choice," said Chet. "You can either empty these or you can put your gear in the truck an' I'll take you back right now. It's your decision. I don't allow no booze in my cow camp!"

It was easy to tell Roger had a hard decision, for him, to make.

"How much longer we got out here?" he asked.

"We should be done by the fourth of July," replied Chet.

Roger was having a hard time reaching a decision. It was readily apparent he liked his booze.

After what seemed like an eternity, Roger

said, "I ain't got no money an' need this job. I guess I can last till the fourth."

He started to raise the flask to his mouth, but Chet stopped him. "No more drinkin'!" Chet slapped Roger's hand, knocking the flask to the ground.

Roger immediately bent down to pick up the flask, but Chet ordered, "Empty it!"

Roger did as he was told.

"Now the fifth!" ordered Chet.

The seal on the fifth hadn't been broken. Ruefully, Roger broke the seal and poured the contents on the ground.

When the bottle was empty, Chet asked, "Is that all?"

"Yep," was Roger's somewhat mournful reply.

"Good!" said Chet. "Now we can all hit the sack."

We all turned in. Nobody said anything about the incident.

The next morning, Roger appeared to be a little nervous. His hands were shaking a little at breakfast and he had to use both hands on his coffee cup to keep from spilling it. Apparently, he'd been taking a sip from his flask to calm his nerves when he needed to. But there was nothing in his flask today.

Noting Roger's condition, Chet roped out a gentler horse for him that day. While the horse did buck some, actually he just kinda crow-hopped around, Roger didn't have to put on a spectacular bronc ride like he did with the other two horses he'd been given to ride.

Roger rode the horse, but when the horse stopped hopping, Roger didn't have that look of satisfaction or conquest on his face like he did with the previous two horses he'd been given to ride.

"This horse don't want to work much this mornin'," he said. His hands were still shaking and he tried to conceal it by adjusting his reins constantly. If someone hadn't known about the incident the night before, they'd probably have thought the horse's crow-hopping had got to him.

Before we started out that morning, Chet asked him, "You all right?"

"Yeah," was Roger's gruff answer.

We started out and Roger lagged behind a little.

Chet, Jim, and Rod were riding beside each other and I was following close behind. I heard Rod ask Chet, "How come you didn't run him off?"

Chet replied, "He's a good bronc rider, one of the best I've seen. I can get some of these tougher horses ridden with him around. I'll keep him if I got all his whiskey emptied out. He should be a pretty good hand when he sobers up. If we can't keep him sober, I'll send him down the road."

"He sure can ride," said Jim. "That Sunset horse is as bad to buck as any horse I've ever seen an' Zipper ain't no slouch."

"We'll just have to see what happens," said Chet. "He's a good enough bronc stomper, I'd like to keep him around, if I can keep him sober."

Rod asked, "What about Clark?"

"He's got a lot to learn an' he sure ain't much of a rider," said Chet. "But he's willin' to learn. He actually thanked me for lettin' him rope. That kinda surprised me. He can be of some help as long as he maintains his attitude."

I again arrived at the conclusion that Chet not only was a tough boss, but he was fair. I thought he might be using some psychology on his hired help.

Chet started sending riders out a short time later. Although Roger lagged behind a little, he kept up. I found out later that Roger and Clark got the short circles and thought Chet wanted to keep an eye on both of them.

Our branding went well that day. When we were done and after Chet had counted ears and entered the total in his tally book, he said, "We'll move camp tomorrow an' we won't have to go so far to start our gather. Everybody all right?"

Everyone nodded, even Roger. He asked the question looking at Roger and sizing up his horse. The horse wasn't covered in sweat and dust as his other two horses had been. Chet grinned a little.

Back at camp, John, the cook, was already preparing to move camp. He'd packed all the groceries except what we needed for supper and breakfast the next day.

Before breakfast, everyone rolled up their bedrolls and put them in the truck. Rod and Stan had been selected to remain behind and help the cook load what he needed in the truck. Rod would drive the truck, as he knew where the next camp was going to be located.

William had the cavy run in and Chet roped out a horse for everyone to move the cavy to new grazing grounds. When he had Clark's horse, he said as Clark haltered him, "I'll help you with this horse."

When Chet went to help Clark, Clark already had the hobbles on the horse. Clark was brushing the horse, although he wasn't really standing for it.

"I'll get him saddled for you," said Chet, throwing the saddle pad, then the saddle on the horse.

When Chet cinched him up, the horse reared back. "I forgot he's a little cinchy. He'll be okay after he's walked around a little. Lead him off for a piece, Clark."

Clark did as he was told and when he was out of earshot, Chet told Jim, "Get on the off side. I'll cheek the horse from the ground an' you cheek him from the off side. We'll at least get the kid on him."

Clark returned and before he went to get on, Chet tightened the cinch and said, "This horse will buck a little, so be prepared. Don't goose him or he'll come undone! Take it real easy with him startin' out an' he'll be okay."

"Sure," said Clark as he pulled up his britches and pulled his hat on tighter.

I could see that Clark was scared to death, but he was going to get on anyway. He put his left foot in the stirrup, adjusted the reins and swung his right leg over the horse. His foot hit Jim's horse on the rump, causing Jim's horse to start bucking.

Jim's bucking horse started Clark's horse to bucking and he knocked Chet down. But Clark was in the saddle. The horse wasn't really bucking, he was crow-hopping and Clark was holding on to the saddle horn with both hands for all he was worth! There was a little fear on Clark's face as he held on.

I was already mounted and went over to crowd Clark's horse so he couldn't move freely. Jim had calmed his horse down and crowded Clark's horse on the other side.

The other hands were cheering Clark on, yelling things like, "Ride 'em cowboy!" and "Stick with him!" Even Chet was encouraging Clark. It was clear that everyone liked Clark.

Jim and I finally got the horse to stop crow-hopping.

Jim said, "He's done now, cowboy. You rode him! You're sure enough a buckaroo now!"

I simply told Clark, "You did a good job!" even though he'd blown a stirrup and just about pulled the saddle apart.

We rode back to the others, where Chet was getting on his horse. When Chet was mounted, Clark said, "This is a pretty rough horse, isn't he."

"Yep," answered Chet, even though any hand

could have got on him without help and could have rode out his crow-hopping without pulling leather.

"What do you call him?" asked Clark.

"We lovingly call him Widow Maker," replied Chet.

I could tell Chet was building up Clark's self-esteem. The real name of the horse was Pumpkin.

We started trailing the cavy to our next camp, with Chet and Jim leading the way. I kept an eye on Clark as we moved the horses. Pumpkin, or that is, Widow Maker had calmed down but Clark kept a death grip on his saddle horn.

I rode over by Clark and said, "That horse has pretty well calmed down an' should be okay the rest of the day. You could probably let loose of the saddle horn you're chokin'."

"But Chet said the horse was known to buck a little," said Clark.

"I think you took all that out of him earlier," I replied.

"Really?" queried Clark.

"I think so."

"Good," said Clark. "My hand's gettin' tired of holdin' on."

"That horn ain't goin' nowhere," I said. I felt like adding, "If it were goin' somewheres, you would have pulled it out earlier this mornin'," but I kept my mouth shut.

Soon, Rod, Stan, and John passed us.

"We'll have your new home set up shortly. Do you want to make reservations now?" asked Rod as they drove by.

"Sure," said Raymond. "I'd like a queen-sized bed, with three pillows. I'd also like breakfast in bed tomorrow, at about, oh, say ten o'clock."

"Your reservation is noted. But I'll have to look to management about the amenities," replied Rod.

They drove through the cavy. It was nice to know that the tents would be set up by the time we got to the new camp.

I was on the outside of the cavy when a mountain grouse flew up. My horse shied, but didn't start bucking. My horse shying caused Pumpkin, or that is, Widow Maker to shy. Clark promptly fell off.

He wasn't hurt and got up quickly. "Chet told me to watch the horse!" he said. "I never should have listened to you!" he told me.

I explained to him exactly what happened and that the horse hadn't bucked. I wasn't sure if he believed me or not and explained the difference between bucking and shying. I also told him that almost every horse will shy when a mountain grouse flies up under their nose.

Clark seemed to accept my explanation and caught Widow Maker. The horse hadn't run off, he was just standing there watching Clark.

Clark got on without cheeking the horse. I wanted to get on one side or the other in case Pumpkin did do something, but didn't get a chance.

Luckily, Pumpkin didn't do anything when Clark got on.

To strengthen my argument, I said, "See. You took all the buck out of him this mornin'! I wouldn't knowingly tell ya somethin' that wasn't true."

Clark seemed to be satisfied. "I guess I got a lot to learn," he said.

I nodded in agreement, choosing not to say anything.

When we got to our new camp, everything was set up. John had some sandwiches made and we had a light dinner. John said, "Supper will be more substantial, but it'll be a little later."

Chet told Jim, "You take William out an' show him where to graze the horses tomorrow an' the night pasture." The new camp also had a night pasture.

Then he told William, "Graze the horses out there till supper time. Keep a good eye on them. This is new country for some of the younger horses an' they may try to go home. Wait till these guys turn their horses loose an' take 'em all out."

We turned our horses loose and William and Jim took them out to graze. Within the hour, Jim returned. He turned his horse loose in the corral at the new camp.

I heard Jim tell Chet, "William is a little un-happy."

"Oh, really," said Chet. "How come?"

"He seems to think that he's workin' harder an' longer than everybody else."

"Oh?" said Chet.

"Yeah," replied Jim. "He says he's up with the cook, out with the horses all day an' he don't get back to camp until after we've all come in. He wants to be a buckaroo rather than a horse wrangler. He says he ain't got the time off the others have got."

"If you don't mind," said Chet, "I'll borrow your horse in the mornin' an' help him gather the cavy. We can have a little discussion."

On the big cow outfits, a buckaroo's string was his. If the cow boss gave one of a buckaroo's horses to someone else, without permission, it was a sign that that buckaroo was being asked to leave. This was true for everybody. It was a matter of courtesy for even the cow boss to ask permission to use a horse in another's string.

"Of course you can use my horse," replied Jim. "He's yours anyway. But I do appreciate your askin'." Jim was grinning when he said that. Chet was grinning at Jim's answer.

Both men knew the ways of the range.

The next morning, Chet and William were saddled up and headed out to gather the cavy as the rest of us went into the cook tent for breakfast.

Roger's hands weren't shaking as much this morning and he could drink his coffee with one hand rather than holding onto the cup with both hands. He did manage to eat something. He was starting to sober up.

When William and Chet returned to camp, we'd all finished breakfast.

"Soon as I eat, I'll rope out your horses for you," said Chet.

It wasn't long before Chet had eaten and was roping everyone's mount for the day. The last horse he roped was Jackknife for Clark.

As Chet haltered the horse, he said, "I've got a special job for you today, Clark. I want you to help William watch the cavy. William's gettin' a little tired an' I want you to help him today. Then tomorrow, I can give William a day off an' you can watch the cavy by yourself. If you can do that, it would be a big help to me. Can you do that?"

"Sure," said Clark. "I'd be happy to."

Chet had roped out a big raw-boned bay horse for Roger. He told Roger, "This horse will buck some, but after he's got it out of his system, he's actually a pretty good horse. He works a rope good an' can turn on a dime."

Chet noticed Roger's hands weren't shaking as bad as they were a day or two before and asked him, "You feelin' all right?"

"Yep," replied Roger. "Never felt better."

Chet grinned. Roger appeared to be entering the world of the living.

Chet saddled his horse and we headed out, leaving Clark to help William.

When we got a little ways away from camp, I heard Chet tell Jim and Rod, "William's not too happy. He thinks he's workin' harder than everyone else an' not gettin' any rest time. I'll give him a day off tomorrow an' have Clark watch the cavy. I think that'll make him happy. I think I've convinced him not to leave. He wanted to roll up. We'll be a man short today, but the man we're short ain't really much help anyways."

"Don't be discountin' Clark too much," said Rod. "At least he's willin' an' he'll do anythin' you ask of him."

"You're right," commented Chet. "But he does have a lot to learn."

"Probably," said Jim. "Anyways, everyone seems to like him an' he ain't made too many mistakes."

"You're right again," said Chet. "Think about it. If all our hands were as green as he is, we'd probably be out on the wagon till winter set in."

"True," said Jim. "Have you noticed Roger? He seems to be gettin' better."

"Yeah," answered Rod. "He don't spill near as much coffee as he used to at breakfast."

All three men laughed at Rod's reply.

"We'll find out how good a roper he is today," said Chet. "I figured it's about time we found out."

"I wouldn't be surprised if he couldn't rope at all," said Rod. "A lot of them top-notch bronc riders don't spend a lot of time ropin'."

"I'd bet he's pretty fair," said Jim. "I think he's an all-around hand."

Chet didn't say anything except, "We'll find out."

Soon Chet started sending out riders with instructions as to where to meet with the cattle they'd gathered. I'd got the middle circle and it wasn't long before I started meeting the big circle riders with their cattle.

When we met at the branding grounds, Chet said, "Roger, you an' Kent rope today. I'll call you in when we're 'bout half done an' Stan an' Al can finish up."

I started in to rope after the others had taken up their position day herding.

SIX

I couldn't tell how well Roger was roping, but he seemed to have about as many calves caught as I did. Leastways, he was dragging a calf to the fire about each time I turned one loose and headed into the herd to catch another one.

When Chet figured we had about half the calves branded, he called us in and had Al and Stan finish up. Roger and I took Al and Stan's positions day herding.

We finished the branding. Chet counted the ears, got on his horse and we headed back to camp.

On the way, he hollered at Roger, "You did pretty good ropin' today!"

"It's been a while since I did any ropin'," Roger hollered back. "I'm really a little rusty. Need more practice!"

"You'll get it," replied Chet.

I heard Jim tell Rod, "That Roger's a better

roper than you thought he was. I told you he was an all-around hand."

"Yeah," muttered Rod. "He'd be a better hand if someone weaned him off the bottle. I'd be willin' to bet when we get done, he goes to town an' ties one on for weeks, even months, maybe even years. He's just that kind."

"I won't take you up on that bet," said Jim. "I think you're probably right. For his sake, I hope you're wrong."

We got back to camp and found William and Clark chatting with the cook in the cook tent. Everybody except Chet turned their horses loose in the night pasture. Chet kept his horse in the corral where Clark had put Jackknife.

"I'll keep my horse in tonight. Maybe Clark can use a hand gatherin' the cavy in the mornin'. How'd he do, William?"

"Near as I could tell, he did fine," answered William. "We didn't lose a single horse."

"That's good," said Chet. "I'll be gettin' you up early, Clark. Be ready."

"Sure," answered Clark.

The next morning, Chet and Clark showed up with the cavy just before we finished eating.

They got their breakfast then Chet started

roping out everyone's mount for the day. He roped Pumpkin for Clark.

"Can you handle him this mornin'?" asked Chet.

"Sure. I handled him the other day, didn't I?"

A signal to Jim from Chet, unnoticed by Clark, and Jim moved into position where he could keep Widow Maker relatively still while Clark got on. Rod noticed where Jim was and moved to the other side of Widow Maker.

As Clark made ready to get on, Jim was saying, "Easy there Pumpkin, easy boy."

Clark heard him and exclaimed, "Pumpkin? This here is Widow Maker!"

"Yeah, said Jim. "I know. I was just … ah, teasin' him. Go ahead an' get on."

Clark got on without any problem.

When Clark was in the saddle, Jim asked, "You got him? He'll probably buck."

"I'm ready," said Clark, gripping the saddle horn as hard as he could.

"Don't goose him, just let him walk out slow," said Jim as he turned the horse's head loose.

The horse took a step then took a jump. Everyone was watching and started encouraging Clark. Clark stayed with the horse on the first jump, then loosened up and started leaning to the right on the second jump. Rod was there and pushed Clark back in the saddle. Clark stayed with him.

After the third jump, Widow Maker stopped. Clark almost went off over the front of the horse, but regained his balance and stayed on. Both horse and rider stayed there, breathing a little heavy.

"Got him topped off, cowboy? asked Chet.

"I think so," answered Clark.

"I think he's done for today," said Chet. "Take out the cavy an' keep a good eye on them today."

"Yes sir!" replied Clark as he trailed the cavy out of the corral.

As we left the camp, Roger asked Chet, "How come you're pumpin' that kid's ego? Anybody could ride that horse."

Chet replied, "Clark's pretty green, but he does have potential. We'll give him all the encouragement we can, but it don't hurt none to string him along. He don't know that we're havin' some fun with him. Don't you clue him in. Raymond, you be prepared to rope a lot. We're gettin' close to your outfit's range an' you'll probably see more of your outfit's cows."

Raymond just nodded.

The day's branding went without incident and, as we headed back to camp, I wondered if we'd have a cavy that night. I didn't put much stock in Clark's abilities.

We got to camp and Clark wasn't in with the cavy yet. William generally showed up about the same time the buckaroos got back. Everybody, except Chet, turned their horses loose in the night pasture.

Chet said, "I'll keep my horse in, just in case I need to go out an' look for Clark."

"That Clark seems to cause you a lot of extra work," said Roger.

"It ain't bad," replied Chet. "It just comes with the territory."

About the time Chet was ready to go out and look for Clark, he came riding into camp.

Chet asked, "Everythin' okay?"

"I don't know," answered Clark. "I think I lost some horses."

"Really?"

"Yeah," answered Clark. "I saw some horses over on another ridge an' went to get 'em, but couldn't catch 'em or even get around 'em. They saw me comin' an' took off."

Chet smiled. "They were probably just rangs."

"Rangs?" questioned Clark.

"Yeah," answered Chet. "Wild horses, mustangs, broomtails. I'd bet you got all our cavy. We'll get a good count on 'em in the mornin'."

"I put the horses I was watchin' in the night pasture."

"Good," said Chet. "You keep your horse in the corral tonight. You an' I will gather the cavy in the mornin' an' William can watch them tomorrow."

"Okay," said Clark.

Chet and Clark went to the cook tent to get something to eat.

"Has your attitude improved William?" asked Chet.

"Yes sir!" replied William. "Catchin' up on a few hour's sleep makes a difference."

"Good. Clark an' I will gather the cavy in the mornin' an' you can resume your job. Clark makes a pretty good horse wrangler. He even tried to get some rangs into the cavy."

"You mean he's out there chasin' broomtails while we're workin' our butts off?" questioned Rod. "He's havin' all the fun!"

Chet grinned. "It appears that way."

The next morning, Chet and Clark gathered the cavy. When the horses were in the corral, Chet told Clark, "There ain't no horses missin'. You did a good job."

We gathered cattle and held a branding that day. When we returned to camp, Matt was there with fresh groceries and mail for those that had mail.

Matt and Chet visited about how things were going out on the wagon, then I heard Matt say, "Your hand, what's his name, Vince? Well, he's got a busted hip. They had to operate an' put some screws in there to keep everythin' in place. I went to town an' picked him up yesterday. He's hobblin' around on crutches at the ranch."

"Worker's comp?" asked Chet.

"Yeah. He'll be on it till he gets better," replied Matt. "You be pretty well done by the fourth?"

"Yeah," answered Chet. "We'll gather the yearlin's after the fourth an' do some cleanup work. Then we'll be done for the season."

"Any of these guys want to help in the hay?" asked Matt.

"I don't know, I haven't asked 'em. Figured I wouldn't ask until we finished our work. Jim, Rod, an' I will break colts this summer. I'm pretty sure Stan will go to town. I'd like to get Roger to help with the horse brakin' but don't know if he'll be sober. He's sure enough a good bronc rider."

"Is he a drinker?" asked Matt.

"Yeah. I caught him with a fifth an' a pocket flask one night." Chet related the earlier incident with Roger. He finished by saying, "He's been off it for a week or so, I don't know, I lose track of time out here. But his hands have stopped shakin'. He couldn't drink his coffee without holdin' onto the cup with both hands."

"I didn't know that when I hired him for you," said Matt. "I'll have to keep a closer eye on that in the future."

"That's all right," said Chet. "We managed to get through it okay. He's a pretty fair roper an' as good a bronc rider as I've ever seen. He rode Sunset into the ground an' Zipper couldn't dump him. He's pretty rough on his horses, but he's eased up since we got him off the bottle."

"He must be pretty good then," said Matt.

Matt ate supper with us that night before he returned to the home ranch. He'd get in well after dark. We might see him one more time when he'd bring groceries and supplies out to us before we returned to the home ranch. We'd be done with the wagon then.

I didn't think about what I'd do when we were done. I was just living one day at a time, trying to do a good job of what had to be done that day. I wasn't making any plans for the future. I was enjoying the wagon. On this outfit, I had a good string of horses to ride, I got along good with the other buckaroos, the grub was good, and the cow boss was good to work for. I was very content. I gave no thought to this way of life coming to an end.

The next day we went on another gather. Chet sent Raymond on the big circle, saying, "We're pretty close to your outfit. You should see a few of your outfit's cows. Keep a close eye on 'em so we don't brand your calves with our brand." He sent Roger to help him.

Chet sent Al and me on the next circle. We both kept an eye on the brands of the cattle we gathered. I only noticed one cow that wasn't branded with our brand.

When we got to our branding grounds, Raymond told Chet, "I've only seen three of our cows with calves. Kent tells me he's seen one. That makes four."

"Your math's pretty good," said Chet, smiling. "But it ain't right. Jim tells me there's another one. That makes five."

"I didn't see that one," said Raymond. Then he added, "I did go to school!"

Chet grinned, then asked, "Did you learn anything?"

"I don't know," replied Raymond. "I do know that I didn't learn how to count cows I ain't seen!"

Both men were laughing.

"I suppose," said Chet, "that's a good thing."

Raymond and Stan roped first. Raymond was careful to let the calves he thought were his outfit's mother up before he roped them and dragged them to the fire.

When he had one of his outfit's calves, he'd tell Chet, "That's ours," and Chet would roll the calf over and draw their brand on the calf. The neighbors branded on the right hip with a Box W. Our outfit branded on the left side with a Flying N.

Raymond's job was a little tougher than ours. He had to look on both sides of a calf to see if it was branded or not. But he did a good job and looked after his outfit's interests well. Generally, the Flying N riders only had to look on the left ribs to see if the calf was already branded. If the calf wasn't branded, our roper would catch the calf and drag him to the fire.

When Raymond was satisfied that his outfit's calves were all properly marked, he told Chet, "I think that's all of ours."

"Good," said Chet. "I'll call Al in an' have

Roger an' Jim rope. Rod can help out on the ground."

Jim had been helping out on the ground and went to get his horse. Chet called Roger and told him, "It's your turn to rope."

Roger entered the herd with his rope down, not giving Raymond or Al a chance to take his position. A few of the cows saw a chance to escape, but I managed to turn them back before they got too far.

The first calf Roger roped was a Box W calf, already branded. When Roger dragged him to the fire, Chet said, "This is the neighbor's calf. He's already branded. You need to look on the right hip to make sure the calf ain't the neighbor's."

As Jim headed into the herd, Chet told him, "Make sure you don't bring in any of the neighbor's branded calves."

Jim smiled and asked, "Do you think I'll need my readin' glasses?

"It sure wouldn't hurt," replied Chet.

The branding went well that day until Roger caught another Box W calf. The calf was dragged in on his right side and Rod didn't notice the brand on the hip. He branded the calf with a Flying N on the left ribs.

When the calf got up, Chet saw the Box W branded on the hip and let out a minor groan and some soft cuss words. He pointed out the error to Rod.

"I didn't even notice," said Rod.

Then Rod said to Roger, "You've caught that calf before. He's the neighbor's! Is that the only calf you can catch?"

Knowing he'd made a mistake, Roger simply said, "He just keeps runnin' into my loop."

Chet was not happy as he made a notation in his tally book that a Box W calf was also branded with a Flying N, although he grinned at Roger's statement. Every outfit took a lot of pride in doing their job properly and this wouldn't stand well with his reputation. While mistakes like this happened occasionally, the cow bosses of each outfit would get together at shipping time and straighten things out. It did make for some good-natured ribbing between the cow bosses, although it was a little embarrassing.

We got back to camp to find that John had a surprise for us. He let everybody eat his fill at supper, then said, as we were leaving, "Hold on! I've got a surprise for you! I baked a couple of apple pies with some apples that Matt had brought from the home ranch. You all want some, don't you?"

He took two pies from the warming oven and placed them on the table.

Jim eyed the pies and said, "You know, I'm plenty full, but I'm thinkin' I could probably make a little room for some of that!"

"Me too," said Rod.

Everyone came back to the table.

"I'll cut 'em so everybody gets an equal share," said John. "I was goin' to make somethin' special for our last night here, but thought I'd better use these apples before they spoiled."

"I appreciate that," said Stan. "I'll take a big piece!"

"They'll all be as equal as I can make 'em," said John.

"He shouldn't get any as much as he slept day herdin' today," said Rod.

"Go to blazes!" exclaimed Stan.

"In fact, don't give him any," continued Rod. "He'll probably sleep tomorrow dreamin' about apple pie an' be in a rotten mood when he wakes up because you ain't there with some!"

"Go to blazes again!" exclaimed Stan. "An' take the express gettin' there!" he added.

We all laughed and even Rod was laughing.

We cleaned up the apple pie in no time. It was a real treat. Who ever heard of fresh apple pie in a cow camp?

The next day it was raining. Chet looked at the sky and said, "I think this is goin' to settle in for the day. It'll be too wet to brand so I think we'll scatter some salt."

Chet roped out everyone's mount for the day then started roping out pack horses. Younger horses and those that were a little on the bronc side were used as pack horses. He asked Roger, "Do you mind if we use Sunset an' Zipper to pack today?"

"Nope," answered Roger. "Might do 'em some good!"

"That's my thinkin'," replied Chet.

Chet didn't bother to ask Clark if he could use Pumpkin. He was a pack horse anyway. Clark was riding Jackknife that day.

Clark noticed Widow Maker being saddled with a pack saddle and asked Chet, "Isn't that Widow Maker?"

Chet, having momentarily overlooked the ruse with Clark, answered, "I need to use Pumpkin, er ... that is, Widow Maker today. We're short of pack horses an' I need him. Packin' salt should do him some good. You don't mind, do you?" In the middle of his comment, he remembered that Pumpkin was Widow Maker to Clark and quickly corrected himself.

"No," said Clark. "If it will help him, go ahead!"

"Later," said Chet, "I'll tell you somethin' about this horse, but we ain't got the time now. Throw a pack saddle on him."

The other hands were saddling the pack horses, but Clark was at a loss with the britchen an' breast straps. Rod went over and helped Clark.

"This breast collar goes like this an' this britchen goes like this," he said as he fastened the equipment. "They help keep the saddle in place. Got it?"

Clark looked over the equipment. "I think so," he said.

Chet and Jim were busy making knots in the horses' tails. We were going to go out head-to-tail tied. Making a knot in a horse's tail required spitting on the tail and knotting it with the lead rope of the horse following. I never was much good at it, so I loaded salt into the pack bags.

There was a mule in the cavy. He wasn't ridden, he was just used as a pack animal.

"I'm told they ride mules on some of the cow outfits in Arizona," I said. "Anybody ever ride this one?"

"Nope," answered Chet. "You want to ride him?"

"I ain't really interested," I replied. "Just makin' conversation."

"Well, stop jawin' an' get him loaded. Two hundred pounds a horse," Chet told us.

When all the pack horses were loaded and tied together, two pack horses for each rider, we started out. Soon we reached a spot where riders could go in different directions. I got the mule and another horse to lead.

Before Chet sent the riders out with the salt, he reminded everybody, "Hobble your saddle horse first, and then hobble each pack horse before you unload any salt. That way, none of the horses will get away from you. Throw out two blocks at each stop. I'd throw two blocks off the gentlest horse first an' make the roughest horse carry the most weight the longest time. Soon as you've got all the salt unloaded where I send you, head back to camp. Don't anybody be bustin' up any pack saddles. Any questions?"

"What if we get lost?" asked Clark.

Everyone laughed. Chet took Clark seriously.

"As you ride out, look behind you frequently. Pick out some prominent landmarks an' remember 'em. By checkin' your back trail, the country won't look so strange to you comin' back. If you ain't sure where you are, in other words, if you're lost, just give your horse his head. He'll bring you back to camp. Horses never get lost. Understand?"

"Yes sir!" replied Clark, somewhat embarrassed at exposing how green he was.

That day, Chet gave Clark the shortest circle. When he sent him out, he said, "You should be back in camp first. If you ain't there when I get there, we'll come lookin' for you."

Clark said, "Yes sir," and left us. He was looking over his shoulder quite often and I couldn't tell if he was checking his back trail or keeping track of where the other riders were. Soon he was out of sight.

"You're takin' a lot of time with that youngster," said Jim.

"Yeah," replied Chet.

"You think he's got the makin's of a hand?"

"Yeah," replied Chet again.

"When do you think he'll be a hand?"

"Don't know," answered Chet. "Now it's my turn to ask a question. How come so many questions about Clark?"

"I dunno," replied Jim. "Just curious."

"Don't you wish somebody had taken you under their wing an' given you some extra time?" asked Chet.

"Nobody did," said Jim, "an' I didn't turn out half bad."

"You didn't turn out half good either," countered Chet.

Both men laughed.

"You're half right!" said Jim and both men laughed again.

"An ol' waddy kinda showed me the ropes when I was younger an' I kinda think I'm payin' back a debt. I'm goin' to send you out next. On your way home, keep an eye out for Clark."

"Sure," said Jim. "Oh, I didn't know you were ever younger!"

Both men laughed.

"To paraphrase Stan," said Chet, "go to blazes!"

Both men laughed again.

"I'll watch out for the kid. I'll do your baby-sittin'.

Jim saw Chet get a look of concern on his

face after he made the last comment, and quickly added, "I don't mind. Besides, I kinda like the kid. Everybody does."

"That's good," said Chet, the look on his face disappearing.

Jim left and Chet and the other riders went out farther. Chet had the riders scatter both to the east and west as they rode north. Chet was leading Sunset and Zipper and he took the biggest circle. Roger was the last rider he sent out before he started to unload the salt on his pack horses. Roger was leading a couple of broncs.

When each rider had unloaded his pack horses, he'd start heading back to camp. The riders started drifting into camp, one at a time. Jim and Clark were the first ones in camp. They'd turned their horses loose and were relaxing in the cook tent drinking a cup of coffee when I showed up. Raymond was already in camp, too. While I unsaddled my horse, Jim and Raymond unsaddled the mule and my other pack horse. Clark was closely watching the unsaddling of the pack animals and how the equipment was stored.

Al got to camp, leading one horse and herding the other one. The horse he was driving went right into the corral. Clark caught him and started to take off the pack saddle.

"You guy's spit ain't no good," said Al.

"Oh really," said Jim. "How come?"

"The knot came undone an' that horse got loose," answered Al. "Couldn't catch him, had to drive him home."

"Why didn't you rope him?" asked Raymond.

"He got loose after I'd unloaded the salt an' I figured a rope swingin' around the other horse would just cause problems. He was headed in the right direction, so I just let him go an' follered him home."

Clark only heard the tail end of the conversation and asked Al, "You got lost out there?"

Al laughed and replied, adamantly, "No! I ain't never been lost in this country! Only a greenhorn could get lost out here!"

The other riders started drifting in.

Chet was the last rider to get to camp. "Everythin' go all right with you boys today?"

Jim answered, "Near as I could tell. Al had a horse get loose, but he followed the horse home. Clark thought he'd got lost. Good thing we tied the pack bags on the sawbucks."

"How'd Clark do?" asked Chet.

"When I came across him, he'd unloaded his salt an' was headed back to camp," replied Jim.

"He didn't get lost then."

"Nope," said Jim. "When I met up with him, he did look a little bewildered, but he was headed in the right direction."

"Good," said Chet. "I saw a lot of Box W cows out there. We got to be real careful brandin' the next few days. Raymond, he'll get a lot of ropin'."

After supper that night, Clark said to Chet, "This mornin' you said you'd tell me somethin' about Widow Maker. What is it?"

"I ain't got time right now," said Chet. "I'm tired an' goin' to bed. I'll tell you later."

Clark didn't say anything and we all went to bed.

The next morning after we'd had breakfast and had saddled our horses, we headed out for another gathering and branding. Chet and Jim were leading and I heard Jim ask Chet, "How long you gonna keep up this ruse with Clark about Pumpkin bein' called Widow Maker?"

"I thought we'd keep it goin' until we got off the wagon," replied Chet. "I didn't want to tell him while we were on the wagon for fear I'd embarrass him."

"I'd tell him now," said Jim.

"How come?"

"He knows everybody here an' gets along well

with 'em. They all like him an' he wouldn't be too embarrassed among friends."

"Maybe you're right," said Chet. "I'll straighten him out next time he asks me."

"Good," said Jim. "If you keep him in the dark too long, it'll be more embarassin' for him."

We made a good gather that day and Raymond pretty well caught all the Box W calves. We didn't put the wrong brand on anything.

After supper that night, Clark again asked Chet, "What were you goin' to tell me about Widow Maker?"

I could see that Chet was a little uneasy about the upcoming conversation with Clark.

He said, "I guess it's about time you knew."

"Knew what?" asked Clark.

"I'm gettin' to that," said Chet. "Keep your shirt on! That horse you call Widow Maker, well ... ah ... he's not really Widow Maker. His real name is Pumpkin. He's actually a pack horse an' don't get used much except for packin'."

"I thought somethin' was funny when you kept callin' him Pumpkin," said Clark. He was starting to get a little red in the face.

"We were just havin' a little fun with you," said Chet. "Bein' kinda green, as you are, I thought I could build up your confidence as you sorta learned the ropes. We've got some pretty tough horses on this outfit an' I didn't want to see you get hurt. A horse like Sunset or Zipper could have put you in the hospital, or worse."

Clark was getting redder in the face and becoming more embarrassed.

"We really, that is, I really didn't mean no harm in it," said Chet. "I actually think it helped you out. Now you can ride Pumpkin when he bucks! I was just tryin' to encourage you a little an' these other boys just sorta helped. We just had a little fun at your expense."

Clark was quite embarrassed and I wondered if he would get mad. I wondered what he would be like when he got mad. Up to this point, he'd been pretty even tempered and easy to get along with.

But he didn't get mad. After he considered the situation, he saw the humor in it and said, "I guess you all had a pretty good laugh at my expense." He smiled a little as he said that.

"Yeah," said Chet. "It was kinda fun. What do you want to call the horse now, Pumpkin or Widow Maker?"

I'd kinda like to keep callin' him Widow Maker," said Clark. "That's the name I got to know him by an' it's sorta stuck."

"Then I hope you don't mind if I keep callin' him Pumpkin an' don't correct myself," said Chet. "At least we'll be on the same page now. I was gettin' kinda careless with his new name an' about blew our joke."

"I did wonder what was goin' on when you had to correct yourself," said Clark.

"Well, there's no harm done," said Chet.

"You haven't changed the names of any of the other horses I ride, have you?" asked Clark.

"Nope," answered Chet. "One was enough. Even with just one, I had a tough time keepin' it straight. More than one would have been too much trouble."

"I guess I could achieve some measure of fame tellin' everyone I rode Widow Maker on this outfit," said Clark.

"You might become infamous tellin' people that," replied Chet. "Remember, he don't buck that hard. I think he'd have a hard time buckin' off a wet saddle blanket!"

All the other hands were gathered around while Chet was coming clean with Clark. When they saw his reaction to the situation, I think it raised their estimation of Clark. They already liked him and now they liked him even more. And, although he was pretty green, there wasn't anything any of them wouldn't do for him. Clark made one final comment regarding the situation.

"Look out now. I'll be lookin' for ways to get even!" he said.

Rod asked, "Now that this situation is straightened out, how are we goin' to have any fun?"

"Be careful," said Jim. "You might be the butt of the next joke!"

"Hum," replied Rod, after some consideration, "I don't think I could take it as good as Clark."

"Don't worry," chimed Al. "We can always watch Stan sleep! I keep wonderin' when he's goin' to fall off his horse sleepin'! That would do for a real good laugh!"

"Go to blazes!" exclaimed Stan.

"If that did happen," continued Al, "it might be funnier watchin' you walk back to camp! I'm sure we'd all enjoy that!"

"Take the express goin' to blazes!" replied Stan.

Everyone laughed and went to bed in a good mood.

SEVEN

The next day went pretty much like the others, gathering cattle, branding, and returning to camp in the afternoon. We were approaching the end and would be returning to the home ranch before long. Some of the fellers were talking about being done on the wagon and going to town for some fun.

I was content to enjoy the days as they were. It was cool in the mornings, but the afternoons were becoming hot. I was glad I had chink chaps for the warmer weather. Rod had shotgun chaps and he wore them every day. I couldn't see how he took it, as hot as the afternoons were getting.

One day, Jim was a little careless getting on his horse and got bucked off, but he wasn't hurt. Al caught the horse for him and as he handed the horse to Jim, Jim said, "I guess I'm gettin' a little old."

"Well, Old Timer," said Chet, "I could always

trade Pumpkin for you to ride. Do you want to ride him?"

Jim laughed. "Nope, I ain't hankerin' to ride no Widow Maker horse."

Clark overheard the talk and said, "I couldn't trade Widow Maker to you. You might get hurt ridin' him!"

Jim laughed. "Are you gettin' even?"

"Possibly," replied Clark.

It was apparent that Clark fit in well with the hands, even though his buckarooing skills were lacking to some degree.

"Do you want me to snub up your horse while you get on?" Clark asked. "Or would you prefer to have a steppin' stool?"

It appeared that Clark could dish it out as well as he could take it.

"I'd prefer a steppin' stool," answered Jim. "Do you have one?"

"I'd have to go to town to get one," replied Clark. "But that would take a couple of days. Can you wait?"

"I don't think Chet would approve of that," said Jim. "I think I can manage," he said, looking around on the ground.

He found what he was looking for, a small flat rock about an inch high and two or three inches across. He took the rock, placed it on the ground next to his horse, put his left foot on it and swung up into the saddle.

"That's all the help I needed," he said when he got his seat.

"I thought I was more help than a rock," said Clark, indigently.

"You are, but not much more," said Jim.

Both men were laughing as was everyone else.

"Leave that rock there," said Jim. "Don't let it get away! I might need it tomorrow!"

We all left camp in a good mood that morning.

Jim was riding up front with Chet and I heard Chet ask him, "Are you all right? That looked like a pretty tough landin' you made back there."

"I'm okay," said Jim. "Did you notice how Clark was givin' me the business?"

"Yeah," replied Chet. "It took him a while, but he's fittin' in pretty good."

"Yep," said Jim.

The day went on without further incident.

The next morning, while Jim was saddling his horse, Clark asked him, loud enough for everyone to hear, "Can I get your rock for you?"

Everyone except Jim was laughing. Jim was taken by surprise, but answered, "Sure."

Clark found the rock and asked, "Where do you want it?"

"Right here," said Jim, pointing to the ground next to his horse.

Clark got the same flat rock and put in on the ground where Jim had indicated. Then he brushed up some dirt around it.

"Is that suitable?" asked Clark.

"That should do," replied Jim. "You know, it's about time I got some of the respect I truly deserve!"

"Yes sir!" said Clark, brushing some of the dirt off the rock.

"You don't ever quit, do you?" said Jim.

"I told you I'd get even," said Clark.

Everyone was watching the spectacle and they were all laughing.

"You know," said Jim, "I don't really need so much attention."

"But you just said you deserve it," replied Clark. "I could even keep an eye open today for a taller rock, if you want one!"

"That ain't necessary!" said Jim.

"Just tryin' to be helpful," replied Clark.

The next few days were really fun. We made our gathers and branded. We all enjoyed the good-natured bantering between Clark and the other hands.

Clark was careful not to joke or tease Chet. After all, he was the boss and Clark wasn't sure how far he could go with him.

Things got real serious one morning when Raymond got bucked off and got hung up in a stirrup. He was dragged about twenty yards. Some of the hands started after the horse, but Chet stopped them.

"Don't chase him!" he hollered.

Roger saw what was happening and hollered, "Roll over on your belly! Roll over!"

Raymond rolled over. I don't know if it was because he was being bounced along on the ground or if he did it intentionally, but his foot came out of the stirrup and he was free. His shirt was torn both on front and back and he'd lost his hat.

"You okay?" asked Chet, as he rode over to where Raymond was getting up.

"I think so," replied Raymond. "This shirt's about had it. Where's my hat? An' my one boot?"

Raymond's boot had come off when he got his foot free from the stirrup.

Stan had caught Raymond's horse and was leading him to Raymond. "Your hat's over there," he said, pointing to the ground about thirty feet to the west. "Your boot is back there."

Al hadn't got on his horse yet, so he walked over to where Stan had pointed and picked up the hat and the boot.

"You've got some pretty bad cuts on your back," said Al. "Better get somethin' on 'em."

Jim went to the cook tent and met John coming with the first-aid kit. John had seen everything from the tent. "This stuff is kinda old. Don't know if it's still good, but it'll be better than nothin'."

Jim opened up the first aid and got a tube of salve and started putting it on Raymond's cuts.

"That smarts!" exclaimed Raymond.

"That's good," replied Jim. "That means it's still good!"

"But it seems like the cure is worse than the injury!" cried out Raymond.

"Hold still! This'll help," said Jim as he applied the salve mercilessly.

Raymond took his hat and boot from Al.

"Thanks," Raymond told Al.

Clark asked Chet, "How come you told everyone not to catch the horse that was draggin' Raymond?"

"That's simple," replied Chet. "If anyone had

chased the horse, it would have become a horse race an' just made matters worse."

"Oh," said Clark. Then Clark asked Roger, "How come you hollered 'Roll over on your belly'?"

"I've done some stunt work in the movies," answered Roger. "When the script called for someone to be dragged, that's what we'd do in addition to havin' a trip wire attached to the stirrup. Occasionally, the trip wire wouldn't work. Also, if you notice, I've got my boots slit from the top down. That makes it easier to get your foot out if you do get hung up. It's pretty handy when rodeoin'."

"You rodeo?"

"Yep," replied Roger.

"I saw your boots were cut down when you took 'em off at night," said Clark. "I didn't think there was a reason for it. I just figured you didn't have enough money to get a new pair."

Roger laughed. "I've got a new pair in my car."

Raymond went to the tent and got another shirt from his bedroll. "Any of you guys need any rags? That's about all this shirt's good for! I hate to waste anything."

Raymond didn't have any takers so he threw the shirt away.

Chet gave Raymond the short circle that day.

We were approaching the fourth of July. Soon our job out on the wagon would be done. According to Chet, we still had some work to do gathering some yearlings, then we'd be done.

One night at supper, Chet said, "We'll make one big gather tomorrow. I don't think we'll have many calves to brand. If we do, we'll make another big circle the next day an' get 'em branded. If we don't get many, we'll break camp an' head for the home ranch."

The next day, we all made big circles. We gathered a lot of cattle, but not many unbranded calves. We got them branded.

At supper that night Chet told everyone, "Tomorrow we'll head to the home ranch. Jim, Rod, Stan, Al, Roger, Raymond, an' Kent can lead the cavy back. William, you an' Clark follow. When you get up, roll up your bedrolls an' put 'em in the truck before you saddle your horses. Jim, if you'll throw the pack saddles on top of the bedrolls, I'd appreciate it. John can start loadin' the groceries, except what we need for breakfast, on the truck tonight."

"I'll give him a hand," volunteered Clark.

Everyone else volunteered to do something to help John that night, following Clark's lead. Stan volunteered to do the dishes, which surprised everybody.

"If Stan's goin' to do dishes, I better dry 'em," said Al. "He's liable to fall asleep an' not get 'em all clean!"

"Go to blazes!" muttered Stan.

"I probably will," said Al. "An' I bet I'll meet you there! It seems to be your favorite spot. You're always referrin' people there!"

"Anyways," continued Chet, "I'll help John get the rest of his stuff loaded an' drive him back to the ranch. Supper will be ready when you get there. There should be plenty of hot water in the bunkhouse for showers, if you don't stand in 'em all night."

The next morning the hands gathered up their personal belongings and stuffed them between the mattress and tarp covering the bedrolls.

"I suppose I'll need to do laundry first when I get to the ranch," said Jim.

"Don't anybody do laundry until everybody's got a shower. There might not be enough hot water to go around," said Chet.

With the bedrolls and pack saddles loaded, we all mounted our horses and started toward the home ranch. William and Clark followed.

They didn't have much work, the horses knew where they were going. The fellers in front had a tougher time, slowing the horses down and not letting them pass us going home.

About an hour after we left, Chet and John came driving through the cavy and us fellers in front had to eat the dust from the truck until Chet and John got well ahead of us.

I made the comment to Rod, "I'm sure glad we didn't have to follow the cavy. Look at all the dust they're kickin' up."

Rod turned around and looked behind him. "Yeah," he said. "It's been quite a spell since we had any rain. Those boys will probably want the shower first, as much dust as their collectin'."

We pulled into the home ranch around three o'clock. We turned the cavy loose in the horse pasture. The feed had grown well during the last few months and the horses would get fat in the coming months.

Vince came hobbling down to the corral on his crutches when we showed up. He was glad to see all of us.

"It's been real borin' here with nothin' to do," said Vince. "They won't even let me ride a tractor around with this busted hip."

"We heard it was busted," said Rod. "I'll bet it was real painful ridin' back to the ranch with Chet."

"Yeah, it was," answered Vince.

While Vince was a nice guy, nobody wanted to spare the time to visit with him. We all wanted to get to the showers and get what we could of the hot water before it was gone. Clark did visit for a time.

Vince said, "You're the feller that replaced me, right?"

"Well," said Clark, "I feel sorry for you, but I'm glad I got a job. I've got to get to the shower before them other guys use up all the hot water."

"I hope you did a good job for me," said Vince as Clark left.

The hands entered the bunkhouse and immediately stripped down and got into the showers. There were ten shower heads in the shower room, kind of set up like an army barracks. The water ran dusty brown as it went down the drain.

Clark was the last one in the shower. When he came out, he said, "You guys didn't leave me much hot water! It was gettin' plumb cold."

Cleaned up, dried off, we put on whatever clean clothes we could find and went to supper.

The buckaroos had their own kitchen and ate separate from the other ranch hands.

"Tomorrow's the fourth," said Chet. "Take tomorrow off, do whatever you want, but be back on the fifth, sober! We've got a few days work when you get back. Then we'll pretty much be done."

I didn't know what to do on the fourth. Some of the boys wanted me to take them to town, but I declined. I knew that if I took them to town, I'd be responsible for them. And I thought it might be a pretty hard job getting them back to the ranch, sober. I decided to stay at the ranch and do laundry. Clark and Roger were the only other ones that stayed at the ranch. All the others went to town.

Raymond went to the Box W.

Chet was surprised to see me in the laundry room when he entered to do his.

"Didn't go to town, huh Kent." It was more of a statement rather than a question.

"Nope," I said. "I ain't much on towns. Roger an' Clark stayed here too."

Chet looked surprised when I told him Roger stayed behind. "I thought for sure Roger would go to town. Clark stayin' behind don't surprise me. But Roger's does."

I asked, "What kinda shape will the others be in when they get back?"

"Jim, Rod, Al, an' Stan might be a little hungover, but they'll be able to work. Don't know about William. He's too young to drink, but there's plenty of places where he can get it."

My laundry had finished drying and I said as I gathered it up, "Think I'll put this away an' take a little nap."

By the next morning, everyone had made it back from town. William had a noticeable hangover, but the others appeared to be okay.

Chet roped out everyone's horse and we saddled up. Matt had a horse saddled and joined us.

As we were leaving, Chet said, "We've just got to gather the yearlin's an' corral 'em across the road. The tractor trailers will be waitin' for us."

Gathering the yearlings was difficult. They didn't want to go. They weren't herd broke. We had scattered out and were combining the yearlings as we neared the corrals. We got to the corrals and the tractor trailers were already there waiting for us. We had the yearlings milling around the front of the corrals. The gate was open, but none of the young cattle had ventured into the corral. Each time they went around, they got closer to the gate.

"Don't crowd 'em!" cautioned Chet. "Let 'em take their time."

Some of the yearlings stopped to look into the corral, but didn't go in.

All of the sudden the air brake compressor on one of the trucks went off, making a loud noise of escaping air. The cattle heard that and it spooked them and they started running. As hard as we tried, we couldn't stop them. I've never seen or been anywhere around a stampede, but I figured I was in one now!

There was no stopping the frightened yearlings. They simply went around us. They were more afraid of the noise than they were of us. We'd gathered about a thousand head and didn't have a critter to show for it when it was over.

Chet went to the truck drivers and said, "You guys will have to come back tomorrow. That air tank goin' off spooked our cattle. Tomorrow, turn off your trucks while you're waitin' for us. We'll have to make another gather tomorrow."

The next day we were up early and had fresh horses. Matt joined us again. I thought the yearlings would be harder to gather, but it seemed like today's gather was easier than yesterday's. We still had a sizeable amount of trouble.

Once again, we had the cattle milling around

in front of the gate and once again each time they went around, they got closer to the gate. As they went around a few entered the corral. Once they started, all of the others followed.

It was a relief when Jim closed the gate and we had the yearlings captured.

Horses were hobbled, chaps came off and we started sorting and loading cattle onto the trucks. There were two loading docks at this set of corrals and as soon as one truck was loaded and pulled out, another one backed into position. I thought the whole operation went pretty smoothly.

It was well after dark when we got back to the ranch that day. But the yearlings were all shipped.

The next morning after breakfast, we were all gathered in the bunkhouse. Chet went to William and asked, "Do you want to help in the hay?"

"No," said William. "I flunked out of college an' think I'll try an' go back an' see if I can better myself. I'll roll up."

Chet then asked Clark, "Do you want to help in the hay?"

"Sure," answered Clark, "I ain't got nothin' better to do."

Chet then asked Roger, "Do you want to help out in the hay?"

"Nope," replied Roger. "I think now that I've quit drinkin' I'll go back to rodeoin'. I used to be pretty fair in the saddle bronc ridin'."

I could see the disappointment on Chet's face. He wanted Roger to help break horses during the summer.

Chet asked Roger, "Do you think you can stay sober rodeoin'?"

Roger replied, "I dunno. I think if I don't drink, I won't get drunk."

"That might work," replied Chet.

Chet came to me and asked, "Kent, do you want to help out in the hay?"

I hadn't given it much thought, but said, "No." I didn't want to have to drive a tractor or a swather or baler around all summer.

"What you goin' to do?" asked Chet.

"I dunno," I answered. "I've heard there's some outfits that keep a wagon out all summer, even into the fall when they're makin' the fall gather. I'll look around an' see what turns up."

"I'll give your time to Matt an' he should have your checks ready in about an hour," said Chet. Then he added, "We'll be goin' out on the wagon again in the fall, along about the first of October.

If you need work then, come back. You'll have a job. If you don't come back in October, come around the first of April. We'll need riders for the spring wagon then."

I rolled up my bedroll and put it in my car. I then went to the barn along with William and Roger to get my saddle. I noticed that Jim, Rod, Stan, and Al followed us.

Probably want to make sure one of us don't steal any of their equipment, I thought, as we walked to the barn. *Well, they don't have to worry about me takin' anythin' that ain't mine!*

Before I got my bridle, blankets, and saddle, I got the blackleg vaccine out of my saddlebags.

"Here," I said, giving the vaccine to Jim, "Give these to Chet. They're the company's. I don't have any use for them."

I loaded my saddle and equipment in the car, shook hands with everybody and drove off. I stopped at the office and picked up my check. It was large enough that I wouldn't have to find work immediately.

I was out of a job again and not knowing what was in store. I was hoping I could get on with an outfit that was as good as the Flying N.

THE END

Other Books by Stu Campbell

Horsing Around a Lot
Horsing Around the Dudes
Humor Around Horses
You Can't Be Serious!
Comedy Around the Corral
More Humor Around Horses
Muddy Waters
Comedy Around Cowboys
The Loner
The Drifter
The Life of a Cowboy
The Wagon

A Young Cowboy's Adventure Series

A Young Cowboy's Adventure
Honey
Surprise!
Intruders
Expectations
Frozen
Advice
Broken
Ginny

Wild Horses for Wild Kids
The Kids Get Horses

About the Author

Stu bases his books on his true-life experiences of ranch life and being a cowboy. He is a graduate of Utah State University with a degree in Animal Husbandry, and has also been a ski instructor, truck driver, and rancher.

About the Cover Artist

Cowboy artist, **R. Loren Schmidt**, is truly a cowboy and an artist. He illustrates from real life experiences from his lifetime of cowboying. A lifetime of dedicated art practice is evident in his expressive and accurate depictions of the contemporary cowboy experience. Loren is most inspired by his friends, horses, and the grand adventures in the backcountry of the West.